In the ...
Of Pioneers

"Grampa, Tell us about the "Good Ol' Days"

Misadventures – Experiences - Life Lessons

Humorous stories of Growing up on a Homestead in the 1950s

With grandsons Grayson & Bodhi

Grade 2 Picture Sept 1956

Brian (Jack) Ash

Dedicated to:

My daughter Bailey – who has been pestering me, since she was seven or eight, to tell my stories. It has taken thirty years to complete the mission but I could not have done it without her encouragement.

My granddaughter, Lydia, re-awoke my desire to pass these stories down. She, unfortunately, passed away at the tender age of three and regretfully, I will never get the chance to tell them to her personally,

My grandsons, Grayson and Bodhi – may their lives be full of love, adventures and their own wonderful stories to tell

Special Thank-yous to:

My sister Linda, who, along with helping to refresh hazy memories, fill in additional details to the stories and her much-appreciated editing skills, have made this a much better book!

My friend Leslie Rutledge who drew the wonderful graphics.

My friend, and co-worker, Marj Hart, who helped edit the stories.

My cousin Teresa, who not only provided many of the pictures but also gave some great suggestions.

An Apology:

To my little sister Linda whom, on occasion, I tease in some of my stories (isn't that what big brothers are for?). In actuality, we spent a lot of time together and got along very well. She is, and always has been, the best little sister I could have asked for!

PS - she made me write this (lol)!

My Sister's Response:

I looked up to my big brother as my "hero" and I believed everything he said. Let me tell you that led me into a lot of situations I should not have been in.

When he said, "Open that little door in the grain bin," I naively did. And I quickly found out what happens. You get a spanking!!! That little door was for the baby chicks to use in spring when the granary is empty. In fall, when the grain bin is full, apparently it lets all the grain pour out on the ground. Gramma and Uncle Paul were not pleased. The only person with a smile on his face was Brian.

When he said Grampa said we could make toffee while Gramma was out, I merrily got out the brown sugar and baking soda and set to stirring the mixture on the stove. Gramma came home while I was doing so, and I got a real lecture about wasting food. (Probably deserved, but I noted that Brian disappeared quickly.)

There was also the time my brother said Uncle Paul wouldn't notice if "we" took some money from Paul's change tray. I should do it as I would be quicker at it. Brian and I sneaked over to the Pharmacy during our next school trip to the Library and "we" spent it. Gramma immediately noticed I had a little oil lamp I didn't have before — perhaps because I put it on a high shelf lit and it made a big black circle of smoke on the ceiling??? Anyway, Brian hid his purchase and, as always, I protected his involvement by taking responsibility. Not that I ever got any thanks from him.

Brian was generous in many ways, however. For example, when I wanted to visit a friend two miles away, Brian said he would come get me on his bike if my friend would double me to the half-way point. The agreed time was 6:00 pm. Well, I arrived (possibly a bit late) but Brian never showed up. So I hitchhiked, at age six. The truckers were wonderful, feeding me cookies and dropping me right at the driveway. That lecture was really BIG!!!!

So, yes, we may have occasionally got each other into trouble, but having your brother as your best friend is unbeatable. Together we invented lots of games, explored our "world" on all-day bike rides, helped each other with chores and school work. Fortunately, we also had cousins, though somewhat younger than us (Owen, Teresa, and Leona across the way and Lloyd, Laura and Joyce in Baytree) to make Sunday dinners and family picnics fun.

Brian has always been the writer and humorist of us two and I, the more sensible one. But, I guess you can tell that by the stories. This book basically tells life as it was. I am so grateful to the extended family that raised us and continued to love us, no matter what mischief we got up to.

Contents

Tell Us a Story

How often have you asked or been asked, "What was it like when you were growing up? Where did you live? What kind of adventures did you have?"

Sometimes these questions were asked out of curiosity or a genuine desire to know, but many times the question came right after we were trying to make a point, or teach a lesson and had said, "When I was your age..." More often than not, what they really want to know is – what kind of trouble did you get into when you were a kid!

Maybe, because I grew up in a place and time that is foreign to my daughter Bailey – on a farm, in the 1950's, dirt roads, no electricity, no running water – she has always been interested in my life back in the 'good ol' days' – especially the times I got in trouble!

So here are my stories – of my adventures, misadventures, lessons learned and the experiences of being an 'Almost Pioneer'.

Special Note: As my grandsons are very young at this time, there is always the possibility that I will be unable to tell them these stories in person, I have chosen to begin with a fictionalized weekend at my home (Grampa Brian) as the setting for my storytelling - set 6 years in the future (2025) when the boys will be the same ages as Linda and I were in these stories, somewhere between 6 and 11 years old. Also, to honor their memories I have included my wife Dianne (RIP) and my Granddaughter Lydia (RIP) as if they were actually there – the way I wish it could have been.

The rest of the stories - are all true. Well, mostly true - some details have been added and conversations have been improvised to provide context but are similar to how they might have been. The incidents themselves all really did happen. Some of the photos are to give a visual representation of what is being described but are not actual photos of ours.

I hope you get a feel of what farm life was like back in the 1950s and maybe even enjoy a chuckle or two!

The Back Story

When my sister Linda and I were about 2 and 3 years old Dad took a vacation from marriage and we went to live with our Gramma and Grampa for about 8 years.

They took good care of us. They were kind and generous, spoiled us rotten – especially Linda, she used to get away with everything. They were good people, the kind of grandparents everyone would want. But on occasion – actually most of the time – Linda would tire them out and they would seek the assistance of additional troops. These additional troops – aunts and uncles - would leave great impressions on us that we still remember today.

In particular, there were two that generated the most influence – Aunt Barbara, who openly showed affection, gave hugs with warmth and tenderness, teased us with a mischievous twinkle in her eye. Though Gramma and Grampa loved us, they were English and did not often display affection physically. Barb took the time to explain about life and how to look at things in a different way. She must have had a

Stan & Barbara 1964

positive effect on Linda too because she was always much better behaved after a trip to Stan and Barbs.

The second, without a doubt, has been the biggest influence in my life – Uncle Paul.

Here was a young man, 28 or 29, single and to my knowledge, no experience in raising kids, who woke up one morning and found a niece and nephew living with him.

He was an easy-going soul, with a quick smile and never had a bad word about anyone and was welcomed wherever he went. Along with a strong community spirit, he was also a visionary and an inventor.

Uncle Paul - Age 70 - No pictures available for the 50's

He took me under his wing and taught me not only numerous life skills but also many life lessons, often without even realizing he was doing so. That became the foundation of who I grew up to be - along with the Lone Ranger, Uncle Paul was, and will always be, my hero!

A Weekend at Grampa Brian's

"What am I going to tell them?" The old man stared blankly down at his almost empty bowl of chicken noodle soup. He scooped up the last piece of chicken and placed it gently on the paper towel with the others. Picking up the bowl he raised it to his lips and drank the remaining broth, playfully slurping the last noodle.

A whimper near his feet drew his attention down to the inquisitive brown eyes waiting patiently beside his chair which seemed to be asking, "Aren't you done yet?"

He had never been a big fan of 'city' dogs – dogs should be out in the country where they can run free and protect you – but this little Shih Tzu-Maltese cross was just about the most lovable dog you could ask for and had brought a lot of joy to Dianne and him.

The moment Brian's hand moved toward the napkin Bella stood up, lifted her ears and the tail started wagging. He gently laid the napkin on the floor and before he could remove his hand the chicken was gone and the wide eyes were staring at him again, "Is that all?"

Opening his hands to prove he was not hiding anything the old man smiled, "Sorry pup, that's all there is – maybe we will have beef and vegetable tomorrow and there will be a bigger share."

After washing his bowl and spoon he headed toward the back deck, stopping beside Di for a moment - she was playing 'Words with Friends' on her computer. "They won't be here for about an hour yet so I'm going to go sit on the deck, enjoy the sun and think of what I should tell them."

Di turned toward him and with a soft smile said, "You know they love your stories. Whatever you tell them will be just fine but," she giggled, "if they start falling asleep you know you have talked too much."

He knew she loved to give him a rough time so he just smiled, "Good point! We will just have to keep their sugar levels up."

With that, he headed out to the deck and settled down into the lounger. The gentlest of breezes warmed by late summer sun tickled the hairs on his arms and he immediately felt relaxed - what a great afternoon!

He had never been a great storyteller   - sure some short anecdotes here and there to demonstrate a point or two or hopefully get a chuckle but a whole day or so of stories, without a book to read from – whew – that was going to be tough – even though they were his grandkids. But Bailey had been pushing him for quite a while now and she had finally put her foot down. "You have been procrastinating long enough Dad. We are coming down this weekend and you are going to do some storytelling!" So this was it – but what and how was he going to tell them?

Then it occurred to him that the grandkids were in that same 7-11 age ranges as when Linda and he were on the farm. Maybe if he told his stories from a kid's point of view they could relate better and find them more interesting.

Feeling more relaxed now he pulled the brim of his hat down to protect his eyes, closed them and quickly drifted off into daydreams of simpler times, not necessarily easier – there were always lot of chores to be done but lots of time for bike riding, swimming, building forts, skating, just carefree days of farm life, you know - the good ol' days'.

Bella's announcing that someone was at the front door aroused Brian from his 'nap'. "Must have dozed off," he thought to himself, "they are here already!"

Hustling across the family room he arrived at the front door the same time as Bailey opened it, "Hello My Dad, good to see you!"

Brian gathered her in his arms and gave her a monster hug and a kiss on the cheek, "You too Sweetie, it has been far too long since our last get together."

Then he heard a young girl's voice "What about me?"

Glancing left and right he pretended to search for whoever had spoken. "Who said that? Where are you?" Then he smiled and looked down at his granddaughter standing right behind her mom.

He stepped to the side of Bailey and squatted down. "Oh, Little One, I could never forget about you! You know, I think you are even more beautiful than your mom was at your age. Come on; give your Grampa a big hug."

Holding her tight he whispered in her ear, "You know you are my favorite don't you?" Lydia nodded and gave him a smile that just lit up her whole face. He gave her an extra little squeeze, "Well that's good because you are. Now go inside and say hi to Gramma Di and let me help your dad."

Peering down the driveway he saw Cory lift the suitcases out of the back of the truck box. "Where are the boys?" he asked with a puzzled look.

Bailey's smile disappeared and the signs of annoyance swept her face, "Grayson is mad at his dad and won't come in – and of course, Bodhi is backing him up – two branches from the same tree!"

Brian looked back at Bailey, "Well you go in and say hello to Di and Bella and I'll see what I can do." He met Cory halfway down the driveway, "Need any help," he asked.

"Thanks, but I got it," he replied putting down one suitcase and extending his hand.

Brian really liked Cory – he had grown up in the same small town where He and Linda and Brian went to elementary school. Bailey had met Cory when she came north to visit her 'dear ol' dad' and spend a week at a bible school with her 'Ash' cousins. By the time the third summer rolled around she had discovered that Cory and her dad had the same middle name (Cecil), their birthdays were only three days apart and that both Cory's and Brian's fathers had the same first name (Reginald). Brian guessed Bailey took that as a sign because once they graduated from school they started dating and had been together ever since. Cory had an easy-going nature, a quick smile and best of all – was a terrific dad – giving his kids all the love and attention they could want – Bailey had made a good choice.

Good to see you!" he said as they shared a hearty handshake. "Likewise," Brian replied, "have a good trip?"

"Yep, not much traffic, trip went quick."

That was another thing they had in common (most of the time anyway) – neither were great talkers, friendly but conversations were normally short and to the point. "Bailey says Grayson is kind of upset with you, what happened?"

Cory picked up the other suitcase and headed for the house giving a wry grin as he went by, "You will find out soon enough, good luck."

Bodhi did not see Brian coming as he approached the side of the truck; he was busy staring over at Grayson.

Caught by surprise as Grampa opened the door, Bodhi gave a little jump. An ear-to-ear big smile quickly followed as soon as he saw him, "GRAMPA," he excitedly shouted while flinging his arms around his neck and giving him a big hug.

"Hey, young Jedi, how wonderful it is to see you! Wow, look at how much you have grown since I have last seen you." Brian smiled and wondered to himself, "Why is that the first thing most adults say to a kid when they haven't seen them for a while?"

His eyes drifted over towards Grayson who was sitting, slouched over, head down, looking straight ahead at the back of the seat in front of him. "What's up G-man?"

Grayson never moved. His eyes were burning a hole in the back of the seat. Brian thought, wow, he must be really mad. Turning back towards Bodhi, Brian asked, "Your brother looks really upset, what's going on?"

"He is really mad at Dad."

"Why?"

Bodhi glanced over at Grayson wondering if he should tell.

"Come on Bo, you can tell me. Maybe I can help."

Bodhi glanced once more at Grayson and after getting no response started talking, "Grayson was showing me a new trick he had learned on his bike and it didn't turn out so well."

"Why, what happened?"

"He told me he had learned to jump his bike so we built a small ramp in the backyard. But our yard is too small and he couldn't get going fast enough to do the jump real good and he lost his balance and crashed into the fence. He bruised his shoulder and sprained his ankle so he has to use crutches for a while."

"Ouch, that must hurt! But why is he mad at your dad?"

There was still no response from Grayson so Bodhi carried on with the story, "Well, when Dad found out about it, he told Grayson that he should have known better and shouldn't be teaching me dangerous stuff like that – and then took away his phone for a week so he had time to think about what he had done. He has been like this the whole trip."

"Ooh, that's a tough one alright! But why are you still sitting in the truck too?"

Bodhi never blinked, "I'm his wingman and we always stick together."

A smile crossed Brian's face, Yep, he thought, two peas in a pod for sure. "That's good; a man always needs a wingman when the going gets tough."

Brian walked around the truck and opened the door next to Grayson. For the first time, he saw the heavily bandaged ankle, "Tough break there young fella." He slowly reached out and put his fingers under Grayson's chin and gently turned it towards himself. "You are not mad at me are you?"

Grayson looked up and slowly shook his head. "And we are still friends aren't we? Grayson nodded yes. "You know, you are not the first person to mess up with his bike and sometimes get into trouble for it – me, more than once."

For the first time, Grayson spoke, "You did?"

"Oh ya, a couple of doozies - tell you what, why don't you come into the house. You don't have to talk to your dad if you don't want to, but we will have some cake and ice cream and then maybe I'll tell you some about my crash and burns. Sound

Ok?"

Grayson smiled, "Ok Grampa, can you get my crutch for me please?"

*****

After some small talk and a good helping of cake and ice cream Brian stood up, looked over at Bailey and gave her a wink, "I promised Grayson I would tell him about some of my bike escapades, and maybe some other stuff, so how about you all move down to the family room and get comfortable while I set up the computer so we can see some pictures of what I am talking about."

Brian moved his computer chair to where he could easily see everyone. "Are you all ready for some stories?" He looked at each one of them individually making sure he got a nod or Ok from each. The last one he looked at was the youngest -Bodhi – who didn't seem to be overly enthusiastic about this.

"Although I have stories for Lydia and I promised Grayson some bicycle crash and burns, how about we start with this one first?" He looked Bodhi square in the eyes, "You know, I wasn't much older than you, in grade one, when I got chased by a bear..."

Bodhi's eyes opened really wide, "You got chased by a real live bear?"

"Yep, true it wasn't a very big bear but it was a real live bear. Would you like to hear about that?"

"You bet Grampa, tell me the story!"

Satisfied that he now had everyone's attention Brian leaned forward, with his hands' clasp in front of him, cleared his throat and began, "It happened one brisk spring morning....."

That's not a Dog!

Even though there wasn't a cloud in the sky and it promised to be a nice day, it was still early in the spring and Gramma wasn't taking any chances. It had been a long hard cold winter and I had missed lots of school – 51 days in total - due to more than my fair share of colds, flu, chickenpox, measles – if it was going around I caught it that winter. Plus, because it was a 4 km walk to school – uphill both ways - I'm kidding of course, but there were 2 hills – both downhill on the way there and uphill on the way back - I was not allowed to go to school if the temperature was colder than minus 25 in the morning.

This morning was much warmer than that but you could still see your breath this early and there were still some snow patches amongst the trees where the sun couldn't get at it – that meant it was still time for rubber boots, thick wool socks, long johns, winter jacket, home knitted wool mittens and my winter hat (the one with the fold-down ear muffs). Yes, I was warm but that is a lot of clothes to wear for an hour's walk.

I didn't complain too much, it wouldn't have made any difference anyway and I was anxious to get going. Because I had missed so much school Gramma had been homeschooling me and, of course, Linda didn't want to be left out so she joined in. But she was a better student than me and could never resist showing off so I was more than happy to get back to regular school.

Most of the time I was alone on my walk - there were a couple of other students further down the highway but because they were much older than me, and could walk much faster, I was well passed their place before they started out. All the other students lived either close to the school or in a different direction.

Actually, I enjoyed the peace and quiet and today was no different. Except for the chirping of a couple of chickadees – no crows, I didn't like crows – the world was still. I kept listening for the chirp of a robin but maybe it was too early for them yet.

As I passed the neighbor's yard, about halfway down the hill, I saw their big black woolly sheepdog playing along the fence line. Figuring I would give him a pet and share some conversation with him before I continued on, I gave a whistle and hollered, "Come here boy!"

When he ignored me I gave a second whistle and shout out – still no response. Well, I thought to myself, I guess he is chasing a mouse or something. By this time I was passed their driveway so I went back to motoring down the road. When I looked back to see if he was still there, I saw him run through the ditch, up on the road and start heading towards me. I stopped and waited for him to catch up. However, as he got closer I discovered that this was not a woolly sheepdog – this was a small black bear cub!

Now what was I going to do – I couldn't go back up the road, and the nearest neighbor was still over a kilometre away. I wasn't worried about him – bear cubs can actually be quite friendly – it was Momma Bear I was worried about. They don't  take kindly with anybody messing with their cubs and if she thought junior was in trouble I was liable to be her breakfast.

With heavy bush on either side of the road, I couldn't tell if she was nearby or not - there was only one thing to do – RUN and RUN FAST! I got my little legs a churning so fast there was a continual spray of mud coming up behind me – which is pretty tough to do when you are wearing boots and packaged like an Eskimo! I kept glancing over my shoulder but he was still there – a few metres behind, just loping along, enjoying the game.

After a few hundred metres I was just about done – gasping and wheezing like an old-timer. I was about to throw him my lunch, hoping that would distract him long enough for me to get away when he suddenly turned off the road and disappeared into the bush. Whether he got tired of being splattered with mud or just thought I wasn't enough fun I didn't care. I was too tired to run any more but I did walk rather briskly the rest of the way to school that day.

Later on that same morning Linda was walking up to see Aunt Barbara when she heard a noise beside her – thinking it was our dog she turned around to give him a pat. Seeing the cub, she, too immediately thought about Mamma Bear and headed back to Gramma lickety-split.

Later, when Grandma escorted Linda to Aunt Barb's they found Barb gesturing for them to quickly come inside. Behind her house was the bear cub and, yes, the very large Momma Bear!! Grandma, despite being city raised, showed she was worthy of the term "frontier lady." She marched over to the bears and yelled and threw sticks at them till the bears ambled off.

I don't think Linda and I were ever in any danger but we both learned to be much more aware of surroundings when we were out walking alone and me, I sure learned –

"Don't holler and whistle at a black sheepdog until I was good and sure it was really a black sheepdog!"

*"I know you want to hear more about bears but first I need to
tell you a little about the family, the homestead and the house
where Linda and I lived and how we got there in the first place"*

Introduction – To the Ash Family

As anyone knows, if you are going to tell a story you must
have a cast and supporting characters. Seeing as there
are no real plots to develop, there is also no need for any in-
depth character studies, so here is a quick rundown on who is
who in the stories-

Time frame: winter of 1955 to summer of 1960

Location: A small farm in Northern Alberta located about
halfway (50 km each way) between Dawson Creek, BC and
Spirit River, Alberta

The Hero: Me- age 7-11,
average size, mostly
quiet, shy, an all-round
nice kid (most of the
time), lord and master
of my territory.

Arch Enemy: Linda,
younger sister, age 6-
10, way too happy,
liked to sing, smart
(always trying to one-
up the hero), could be
feisty when riled
(which I tried to do whenever I thought I could get away
with it)

The Sidekick: Skipper, medium-sized dog, mutt, like a Border Collie-brown & black - constant companion and protector from wild beasts.

Stan, Reg, Grampa, Gramma, Joan, Paul
(Picture taken in 1965 – 5-8 yrs. after the stories)

Cecil: (our Grampa) - Head of the household – late 60's, 6'0", slim, had a glass eye, true Englishman, didn't talk much but when he did you listened.

Lillian: (our Gramma) - true head of the household — middle 60's, 4'11", hard worker (you were either helping or you stayed out of her way), wonderful, caring lady with heart of gold but you didn't want to cross her.

Reg: (our Dad) (Divorced) oldest Son — middle 30's, 6'1", slim, tinsmith, reserved, good with numbers – *the 'planner'*

Aunt Joan: (Uncle Albert) - daughter– middle 30's, farmers, lived in Baytree AB (25 km west). 3 young children – Lloyd, Laura, Joyce, strong church and community members

Uncle Paul: (Single) - middle son– lived with his parents on the homestead, early 30's, 5'7", farmer, gentle soul, well-liked, churchgoer and strong community member – *the 'doer'*

Uncle Stan: (Aunt Barbara) - youngest son– early 30's, 6'0", farmer, lived just up the road, 3 young children – Owen, Teresa, Leona, churchgoers and strong community members, smart/knowledgeable – *the 'organizer'*

The Old Homestead

As you broke over the top of the hill and the valley opened up in front of you with the Saddle Hills on the horizon it was very easy to miss the driveway into the homestead.

If you glanced out of the side window of the truck you could see the house peeking through the few spruce trees, poplar and birch trees, and small under-brush that protected the yard from the highway.

This part of the country was so far out of the way that most of it had only ever been seen by the Native Americans but most of them had moved on. My grandparents were true pioneers!

When they arrived in Gordondale in 1930 there were no roads, almost no houses and only a handful of people. They had taken the train from Calgary to Spirit River and then rented a couple of horse and wagon teams to take them, their four kids and their meager possessions the rest of the way.

A series of trails that were hacked out of the bush for a proposed railway, that never was built, provided an adventurous last leg of the trip. Rough uneven ground made traveling tough enough but when you added in existing mud holes, leftover pieces of trees that had been used to free previous bogged down wagons and navigating the ruts they had left behind it was a slow journey. There were a couple of way stations along the route where they could overnight and water the horses. It took almost four days to travel the 50 km to their new home about 12 km east of the community of Gordondale.

The six of them lived in a tent for the first winter. By the next summer, they had cut down enough trees to build a small log house. It had dirt floors and windows made out of plastic – just clear enough to let some daylight shine through.

Seven years later the community of Gordondale wanted to start a school but didn't have enough kids living within a 7 km radius of where they wanted to build the school to qualify for a government-paid teacher. With my grandparents, four kids they qualified, so with some encouragement and help the family packed up and moved to the new homestead – on the hill about 4km east from where the school was to be built. This is where Linda and I spent our preteen years.

Linda and I weren't born there – I was born in Peace River about 200 km to the northeast. Linda was actually born on my mother's farm near Grimshaw. We showed up at the homestead a little bit later after our folks separated. Dad packed us up and dropped us off, in Gordondale, at Gramma's and Grampa's until he got things sorted out – I'm not sure how excited they were, being in their early 60's, for a one and a half-year-old and an almost-three-year-old to come and live with them – especially Linda – she was always asking questions and getting into things she shouldn't have. Me, I was the easy one, they would just 'shoo' me out the door and tell me to go play with the dog or bug Uncle Paul – which I was more than happy to do.

Now I don't remember much of the first three years but Gramma must have kept us busy - by the time I was six both Linda and I could read and write and knew our 12x's table. Linda had calmed down some and actually was quite helpful for Gramma.

And me – well the dog and I had explored just about every inch of our outdoor 10 acre paradise, as long as we could still see the house, and we didn't go into the bush – there could be bears, moose, coyotes or other wild animals lurking about – which we saw quite often.

To the south of the house, a narrow band of trees and bush separated the yard from the main road. You couldn't really call it a highway – it was barely wide enough for two cars to go by each other. Everybody drove down the middle of the road. Whenever you met another vehicle both of you would ease over just enough for you to pass each other. There was a lot of clay mixed in with the dirt and not much gravel, so when it rained the road could get very slippery and it was quite easy to slide into the ditch.

It would not be long until there was just one set of ruts, about 6 inches deep right down the middle of the road. Now when you met another vehicle it became a test of skill and judgment. First, you would slow right down and then

Was improved when we lived there

gently nudge your tires out of the ruts, and move slowly toward the edge of the road until your driver side tires dropped back into the right-hand rut – the other driver would do the same. Once you had slowly gone by each other you would then gently nudge your vehicle back into the two center ruts.

The year Linda started school they built a new gravel highway (it wouldn't be paved for another ten years or so) that was much wider and much easier to drive on – especially when it was wet. Although people still drove 'farmer style' right down the middle of the road and still slowed down when you went by someone – you didn't want to throw rocks and break their windshields! Plus gravel roads kick up a lot of dust and if you went by too fast the other driver would not be able to see where they were going.

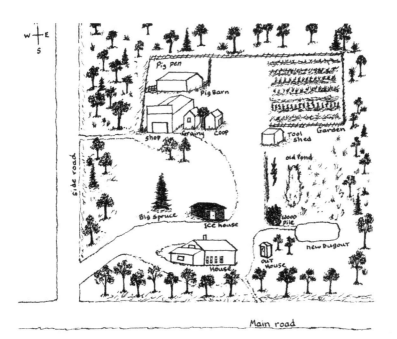

Our driveway was on the south-west corner of the homestead and joined a small range road, with a field on one side and a band of trees and bushes that separated the road from our yard.

As you drove down the dirt driveway you went past the row of trees and bushes, with a large spruce tree and ice house on the left and the house on the right. If you didn't stop at the house, a large woodpile in front of you forced you loop around the house to the right and back onto the main driveway or turn left towards the chicken coop.

At the end of the driveway, a narrow path continued on between the woodpile and the crystal palace (outhouse), over a slight knoll, to the dugout (or dam, as we called it) beyond and what used to be a small pasture for the horses and cows.

If you turned left you would go passed the remains of a wooden fence –on your right that surrounded the barn (now torn down), a small tool shed and arrive at a large garden area. Across from the tool shed and garden (to the west) was the chicken coop, a granary, and a new shop, where Uncle Paul could work on his equipment. Behind the chicken coop and granary was an old pig barn and pen.

By the time Linda and I got old enough to remember stuff, the horses and cows were gone. There were pigs for a couple of years until we ate them, but there were always chickens - lots of chickens and then even more chickens – until we ate them too!

The Farm House

Original Homestead Log House

When Linda and I first arrived at the homestead the backside of the house (facing the highway) looked like the photo above. The window on the left of the house was where Grampa's chair was. The middle window is across from the doorway and the one on the right was their bedroom window – next to the stairway.

By the time we were school age, a porch/shed had been added on and the house had been covered in asphalt siding (photo next page). The window (front center) was where the dining room table sat. An antenna sat atop the long pole so we could pick up the Grande Prairie radio station.

A	SEWING MACHINE STAND
B	CABINET
C	BOOK SHELF
D	STAIRS
E	DRESSER
F	WATER BARREL
G	FIRE WOOD
H	VEHICLE BENCH SEAT
I	ROOT CELLER DOOR

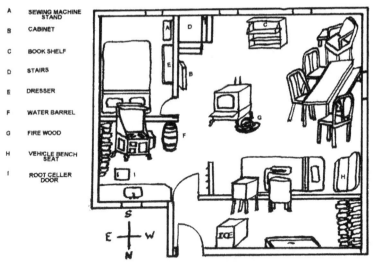

The only entrance to the house was on the north side of the building and at the end of the porch that ran just over halfway up the length of the house. As you approached the door, the first thing you noticed, was a large brass doorknocker (shaped like a lion) that Grampa had brought from his home in

England. As you entered the porch there was a place to hang your coats and an area for your boots. Straight ahead was the door to the house.

To the right of the kitchen door was the washing machine and against the far west wall was where the chopped wood was stacked. To the right of the porch door was the Ice Box (like an early refrigerator - a block of ice was used to keep the food cool). The remaining area/walls held household tools, tubs, pails and whatever else that was thought to be needed.

As you stepped in the main house a counter, with a face wash basin, was on your immediate left. Beyond that was the kitchen window in front of a small kitchen sink, with a slop pail underneath and finally two cupboards. Wood, for the stove, was stacked along the east wall. Across from the sink was the wood-heated kitchen stove similar to this picture.  A reservoir on the right-hand side kept the water warm for washing and shaving. Racks above the stove were for baking – place to let bread rise and pies cool – one of the first things I checked out when I entered the house – might be cookies or pies that night!

On one side of the stove was a trap door that led to the root cellar below – filled with canned moose meat, fruit and pickles. Bins held potatoes, carrots, turnips, and other hardy vegetables. Behind the stove was the wall to Gramma and Grampa's bedroom. On the other side of the stove was a large water barrel – used for drinking and cooking.

Directly across the room from the doorway was a window. To the left was a very narrow, steep stairway up to the sleeping areas for Linda, me and Uncle Paul. In the middle of the wall was a homemade bookshelf that went up to the ceiling. The bottom portion had a fold-out portion that could be used as a writing station. At the end of the wall was Grampa's side table and a comfy chair.

To the right of the entrance was a small partition that hid the view to the day bed/couch behind it. Almost in the middle of the room was a wood heater, to keep us nice and cozy, and a small wooden box that held kindling and the day's wood supply.

Finally, at the end of the room was the kitchen table – bench seating ran along the back of the table (under the window). The coal oil lantern hung above the table.

It wasn't a big house but it was comfortable and we liked living there – except that during the winter we were forever adding on or taking off sweaters depending on when they last added wood to the heater!

"Now that you have the layout of the land you must be thinking – enough of this, it must be about time for another story about bears!"

"I do have another story about a bear – a big, big bear – but first let me tell you about my school, as that is where it happened"

Country School

Sunday School Class 1963

Gordondale consisted of, a small grocery store with a gas pump, a post office, a 10-12 seat eatery – all of which were attached to the owners' homes. There was also a church, 3-4 houses and a community hall with a high rounded roof (like a barn).

The school was built in the bush, down a narrow dirt road about 3/4 km south of this community. Why there? Because one of the farmers further down the road had donated the land to the community.

Enough land had been cleared for a schoolhouse, a 2-room teacher's living quarters, a ball diamond, a grazing area for the horses (yep, some of the kids rode horses to school), a horseshoe pit and enough room for parking when the July 1st picnic was held. The land was surrounded by a 3 strand barb wire fence – either to keep the cattle out or the kids in – maybe both!

The teacher's house sat in corner of the property closest to the road. The schoolhouse was about 1/3 of the way back from the road. The ball diamond, with a wood and wire backstop, was behind the school (very important info as you will find out in the next story).

School Teacher's House

A row of large windows and the only door faced the road. A small, two-pane, window faced the ball diamond. When you entered the school there was only one room. At the back by the door was a place to put your boots and hang your coat. A wood heater was about 3/4 of the way across the room with a stack of firewood against the far wall. The wooden desks were faced towards the blackboard at the front of the room. There were 4 rows of 5 desks. Students were seated in order of what grade they were in.

As there were only 2 of us in grade one, we sat in the first 2 seats of the left-hand row. Behind me was the lone kid in grade two, no one grade 3 so it was an empty seat and our row was filled out by the lone person in grade 4. The other students were spaced out across the room with the grade 9's on the far right. One room, one teacher, 12-14 students, and 9 grades –no wonder teachers never lasted more than a year or two!

Because Gramma had taught us so well I more or less breezed through grade one. I actually spent more time paying attention to the lesson the one grade 2 student, behind me, was getting than on my own lessons.

However, I did get caught cheating once. Now...Now...I

know what you are thinking, but you got it all wrong. I didn't cheat to get the right answers; I cheated to get the wrong answers. "What do you mean," you ask?

The girl in front of me had not received the same level of homeschooling that I had and had to work harder at her lessons. Her weakest subject was spelling – she would always get 3 or 4 wrong, whereas I very seldom got more than 1 or 2 wrong.

I don't know what possessed me that day but I was feeling bad that she never got the best grade so I decided to blow the test. Nothing obvious of course, messed up an 'I' before 'E', left out the 'U' in neighbour, put in an 'O' instead of an 'A' in a couple of words – they were easy enough mistakes to make. I spelled 5 words wrong figuring that would be enough for her to get the best mark that day. It was!

What I hadn't counted on was that the teacher did some figuring on his own and knew exactly what I had done. He kept me after school and explained to me that I was not helping her by giving the wrong answers – it was up to her if she wanted to get better grades and it did her no good if I lowered my scores. And then he gave me another test to do – I never fudged a test again.

I don't know about the other grades but most of my day was doing the 3 R's – reading, 'riting, and 'rithmetic – and of course – spellin'. I learnd reall good – didn't I?

"I also learned – you never help anyone, including yourself, by cheating, whether you have good intentions or not!"

The Big, Big Bear

Did you ever look back at something you had done and wonder, "Was that the bravest thing or dumbest thing I have ever done?" Well, this was going to be my time and I would ponder for the rest of life whether I was brave or just plain dumb? I'll let you decide.

A couple of months after been chased by the bear cub I got to meet Poppa Bear.

Because our school had no electricity and no heat someone always had to show up a half-hour early and light the lamps (during the winter) and start the fire in the big wood heater. Sometimes it was done by the teacher but most of the time it was done by one of the male students on a rotating schedule or when somebody misbehaved or broke a rule and this was part of their detention.

As I had missed so much school that winter and was not only the youngest but also lived the farthest away I had escaped this wonderful chore up until now – today it was finally my turn. I had been shown how to build the kindling sticks and cross piece the cut wood so the fire would start and build real good. One of the older boys helped me practice for a few days by teaching me how to keep the fire going throughout the day. Once he satisfied I knew my stuff he gave the teacher the thumbs up and I was good to go.

I admit I was a little nervous that morning but I was ready to accomplish my mission. Other than maybe walking a little faster it was the usual, peaceful and quiet walk, no cars, no sign of any life, just a dog barking here and there and the chirping of the birds.

I knew I was just about there when I could see the teacher's white shack peeking through the trees. Just as I passed by it and the school came into view I heard a loud grunt! Looking across the yard I saw a big black bear, the biggest bear I had ever seen. He was standing on his hind legs and with his huge, massive claws scratching at a post in the middle of the ball diamond's backstop.

I stood frozen in my tracks – now what was I going to do? I quickly figured out I only had 2 choices: Attempt to climb over the fence - without ripping my pants on the barbed wire (Gramma would not be happy at all about that) and risk detention (so many times the fence had been broken by students that it had become a major offense to use it as a shortcut and could result in serious detention time) or -  walk the 40 metres to the main entrance and then make my way back the 40 metres on the other side to the teacher's house.

What was I going to do? What was I going to do? I just couldn't decide and was just about ready to do 'Eny, Meeny, Miny, Mo' when another grunt and loud snort helped me make my decision real quick. The bear hadn't noticed me yet so I chose, in my great wisdom, to use the main entrance.

Walking very slowly so as not to get his attention I inched my way down the road. I was about 3/4's of the way there when I discovered that the bear was now hidden behind the schoolhouse and I had no idea where he was. I sped up a little bit, doing my best not to make any noise, scurried through the entrance and began making my way back along the fence line.

When I got to where I could now see him again I went into stealth mode and watching every move this big bear made, crept towards the safe zone. I was about halfway there when he either smelled or heard me and dropped down on all fours and turned towards me. I knew at this time that if he charged me my days of being a number one fire starter were probably over.

He stared at me! I stared at him! Neither of us moving we both stared at each – for what seemed to an eternity. Maybe he figured I was too small to bother with, or, was probably not good eating but he finally turned around, stood up, and went back to clawing the post.

Once again I began inching my way forward. Now that he knew I was there I didn't want to startle him and give him any reason to change his mind about eating me! Two hours later I finally reached the teacher's door, I'm kidding, it only felt like two hours! I gave a quiet little knock – no answer – I knocked again, a little louder this time – still no answer. I knocked a third time, a little more persistently – this time the door opened. There stood my teacher, half-dressed, a razor blade in his hand and shaving cream all over his face. "What is it," he asked?

"A bear," I whispered. Looking somewhat annoyed he again asked, "What did you say, I couldn't hear you?"

My voice still shaking I repeated, a little more loudly this time, "a bear, a big, big bear" and pointed towards that backstop.

The teacher looked at the bear and without a word turned around and went back into his house. "Just great," I thought, "It is just me and the bear all alone together again." A few seconds later the teacher reappeared, this time with his rifle. He loaded a shell in the chamber and raised it partially up his body.

Then he gave a loud sharp whistle. The bear stayed standing but turned his head towards the noise. The teacher whistled again. Just a note here – you don't want to shoot an animal in the back. You may not hit any vital organs and you might just wound it leaving a very mad and dangerous animal wandering around in the bush. The teacher was trying to get the bear to face him so he could get the best shot off.

The bear dropped down on all fours, turned and made a step towards us. The teacher raised his rifle to his shoulder. He paused and mumbled, "The scope is out of focus, I can't see him." He raised his trigger hand to adjust the scope. The bear took another step.

"What the..." the teacher annoyingly mumbled. He lowered the rifle and looked at the end of scope – it was covered in shaving cream. I guess when he raised his rifle to his shoulder his forearm had brushed his face scraping off some foam. When he went to adjust the scope this foam had transferred to the scope.

Clearly frustrated and with both us getting a little anxious he quickly grabbed a corner of his undershirt and desperately tried to wipe the lens clean. I'm still watching the bear – ready to jump inside the house if he continued to advance. However, as soon as the teacher lowered his gun the bear stopped, figured this was a good time to escape and took off at a dead run into the bush.

The teacher let out a sigh of relief, "Whew... that was a little exciting wasn't it?" He then looked down at my hands, "Let's see them. Did you cut or scrape yourself climbing over the fence?"

"No sir," I answered, "I didn't climb over the fence."

"Well, how did you get to my door then?"

So I proceeded to tell him about not wanting to get into trouble and had wanted to do the right thing so I had taken the long way around. He slowly shook his head back and forth as he listened to my story.

When I was finished he put his hand gently on my shoulder,

smiled and softly said, "Well that was a brave thing you did - now go start the fire. Then he added,

"Sometimes it is OK to break the rules, and this was one of those times! "

Ok Grayson, here are some bike stories for you – I know how impatient you can get at times so first here is -"

A Long Summer's Morning

(A lesson in Patience)

Not every day can start by being chased by bears. Once school was finished for the year and July 1st picnic was over there could be many days of summer that were downright boring – just the same old stuff day after day. Who knew that by sundown of this warm sunny summer day that my life would be changed forever?

It began as a normal day, well almost a normal day –Linda, and I were allowed to sleep in a little extra, not much, but enough to make it seem like summer vacation had actually begun. After breakfast, it was chore time – feed the chickens, gather the eggs and chop some firewood. On some days I would also have to help tend the garden – you know, the fun stuff, weeding and watering – but this was not one of those days so now I had to find something to do.

When Uncle Paul was around I would wander over to where he was to see what he was building or fixing. Now, being only eight I wasn't all that great of a helper but I was a pretty good fetcher of things and a really good watcher. But today he wasn't around. "Where's Uncle Paul?" I asked Grampa.

He looked up from the book he was reading and with a twinkle in his one good eye and a mischievous smile he said "Had something to do, should be back soon," and with that, he went back to reading his book. That was it! No details! Nothing!

What is he doing, I wondered? If he had gone to town for parts Grampa would have said that. And normally, if he was just going down to the store or visiting a neighbour he would have taken me along. I headed towards the kitchen hoping Gramma would shed some light on the situation. She just gave that same mischievous smile and shrugged her shoulders. Linda was playing with something and was totally ignoring me so no sense in asking her. Well, 'soon' to an adult is not the same as 'soon' is to a kid. 'Soon' can seem like a long, long time.

What was I going to do until he got back? I headed outside, looked around the yard to see if anything looked interesting and finally decided to wander out to the road (2 lane gravel highway) to see if I could see him coming. Of course, Skipper, our dog, joined me on the walk. We had no idea what kind of dog he was, just a dark brown and tan, friendly, medium-sized mix of something, but he had a bark that sure let you know when someone or something, like a bear or moose, was in the yard.

As I moseyed along (that's cowboy talk for walking slowly and not always in a straight line) I peered here and there through the underbrush, searching for any signs of grouse or prairie chicken, or sometimes even a rabbit, that might be trying to hide from me – nothing today. I turned my gaze higher up in the trees to see if I could find a squirrel, a robin or anything that I could maybe throw a rock at – nothing! It was just a quiet and peaceful morning until "Caw, Caw," from a very large crow that swooped overhead and landed in a nearby tree, just outside of rock-throwing range.

I was just about at the side road so I ignored him and turned my attention to where I was walking. The side road went north passed one of Uncle Paul's fields, through a low lying area, passed the bushes where we would pick blueberries or saskatoon berries and up a small hill to another farm about a kilometre and a half away. There was no dust haze hanging around the road or over the valley so I knew no traffic had traveled over it this morning – Uncle Paul hadn't gone this way.

We lived just below the crest of a hill so when you looked up the highway you could only see a couple of hundred metres but when you looked down the hill, to the west, the valley opened up all the way to the Saddle Hills - almost 5 kms. Because it had been hot and dry you could see a cloud of dust in the distance  before you could actually see what was traveling on the road. On busy days, with no wind, the dust would just hang over the road and it was tough trying to figure out what was coming until it got to the bottom of the hill. But today there hadn't been much traffic and a slight breeze had blown the dust into the trees alongside the road and you could see all the way to the horizon. I looked up the road – nothing! I looked down the road – nothing! Now what?

I stood there for a few minutes scuffling my feet in the dirt and half-heartedly kicked at some stones.

I turned my attention back to the highway and hopefully looked both ways – still nothing. Where could he be I wondered? What's taking him so long?

What should I do next? The crow had flown away and it was no fun throwing rocks at empty fence posts. Skipper had deserted me. I could see him chasing butterflies, bounding up and down in the tall flowers and weeds that grew alongside of the road and in the ditch. And then I heard it – the sound of a motor. It was coming from the east. I stared intently towards the crest of the hill – then I saw it – a plume of dust rising just over the horizon. Was it Uncle Paul? If it was, he should be slowing down by now. I listened intently – there was no change in the hum of the engine. Come on, slow down, I pleaded to myself – then the car broke over the crest of the hill – it was just a neighbour. My heart sank but I weakly smiled and waved as he went by. He gave a toot on his horn, waved back and disappeared back into a cloud of dust.

As I stood there watching him drive down the road I suddenly realized I could feel the wave of dust particles settle into my hair and onto my face. I watched it settle over my shirt and pants forming a thin tan layer. Maybe I had stood just a little too close to the road! I gave my pants a couple of smacks and then my shirt – little puffs of dust flew from wherever I hit. Then I violently shook my head while vigorously running my fingers through my hair to get out as much dust as possible. Next was my face. Not quite as simple – seeing as the day was already quite warm as small beads of sweat made the fine dust particles cling to my face. I could feel them in the corner of my eyes, up my nose and on my lips.

I reached into my back pocket for my handkerchief but, as per normal, I didn't have one. So I licked my fingers and gently using my fingernails dug the particles out of the corner of my eyes. If your lips are dry what is it that you do? Lick them of course! So that is what I did. Then it dawned on me – dust is ground-up rock and tastes just as bad as dirt. Not wanting to swallow this 'wonderful' stuff I quickly spit it out and wiped my lips with the back of my hand – which I promptly wiped off on my pants. Now that my lips were clean it was time for the nose.

The natural thing to do is to wipe it on one's sleeve, but I had learned better than that. Washing clothes was a big chore and both Linda and I had been encouraged to try and stay as clean as possible – which included not wiping runny noses on your sleeves - that was what handkerchiefs were for! Which I didn't have! That meant – licking my finger and thumb and then squeezing my nostrils between them and then wiping them off on the grass. It took three tries but my nose finally felt clean again – then I wiped my fingers on my pants, but down near the bottom so hopefully Gramma wouldn't notice. As the rest of my face did not feel too bad I decided to leave it until I found some water.

I took one last look down the road, watching as the cloud of dust stirred up by my neighbour's car settle back down on to the road. There was still no sign of anyone else coming so I decided to walk down the side road and go into the yard through the back path. I gave a short whistle, "Come on Skipper," I shouted. I saw him bounding towards me so I took off running as fast as I could to see if he could catch me – which he did very quickly, flying by and heading into the yard – leaving me gasping for breath in his rearview mirror.

Shop was new when I was there

I slowed back down to a walk and made my way through the back path to Uncle Paul's shop. It wasn't really a path, more of an open non-treed area that Uncle Paul would use once in a while to bring his farm equipment in and out of the yard. There was a couple of small boxes just outside of the shop entrance that I didn't remember seeing before so I peered into them so see if there was anything interesting – there wasn't – at least not today, just a bunch of nuts and bolts and odd parts that I didn't recognize.

As I moseyed by the chicken coop I kept my eyes peeled for

the rooster. He was kind of mean and had a habit of sneaking up behind me and pecking at my ankles.

He was nowhere to be seen so I went back to 'piddling around'. I wasn't sure what 'piddling around' meant but whenever Linda and I would avoid doing our homework, chores or something we didn't like, by trying to look busy doing anything other than what we were supposed to be doing, Gramma would always sternly say, "Quit piddling around and get back to your work." Even though I didn't have anything specific I should have been doing at this moment I was just drifting from here to there without doing much of anything, so I guess that would be kind of 'piddling around'.

Eventually I 'piddled' my way over to the old dugout. That was where we used to get our water from until the new dugout was put in when the new highway was built the year before. Weeds and flowers had sprung up around most of it and a number of small willow trees were now taking over at one end. Bulrushes were growing close to the shore and were rising three feet above the water.

Although I had no idea what they were, and really didn't care, many other types of plants and flowers floated on the surface of the dugout. There was one spot about halfway around, just before the bulrushes, that was my favourite. The bank was a little lower there and close to the water. I had cleared out most of the weeds during previous visits and when I lay down I could peer right into the water.

Early in the spring, it was a good spot to watch tadpoles swimming about but now they had grown into frogs. Frogs are kind of skittish; they only seem to croak when it is peaceful and quiet. Any kind of sudden noise and it was instantly quiet except for maybe one - who must have been the lookout – he would croak every so often until he determined the coast was clear.

But today they were croaking and I wanted to see how close

I could get before they discovered me and quit. Skipper was lying in the shade of the house so I was on my own. Taking very small steps and making sure I didn't step on any dead twigs I moved at a snail's pace along the bank of the dugout. Every time they went quiet I stood as still as I could for two to three minutes until they started up again. During my frequent stops, I had plenty of time to watch the water bugs skimming across the glass-like surface. Bees flying by would swoop down to check out the flowers and then move on. Mostly there were dragonflies - dozens of them – looking for flies, gnats, mosquitoes, smaller dragonflies - pretty much anything that was flying about that they thought were good to eat.

Eventually, I made my way to my spot. My mission was only partially successful – only two frogs were still croaking – most likely the lookout and his buddy. I squatted down next to the dugout and gently brushed through the grass growing at the water's edge. At first, I spotted just one small frog hiding under a leaf, then another by a dead branch, and another swimming just under the service. I must have made a noise or moved too fast because the one by the dead branch made a big jump, for a frog, and then, sploosh he was gone. Within a few seconds, a whole bunch more had joined him – all feverishly swimming out of my view.

I stared at the water for a few more minutes and just about the time that I was wondering what to do next; out of the corner of my eye, I saw a blade of grass move. As I turned my head to check it out, a small frog made a desperate leap for the water. With blazing speed, my left hand shot across my body and I'll be doggone if I didn't catch him in midair. Now what was I going to do – I had never actually caught one before. As I sat there pondering, and the frog looking back at me, I heard Gramma call out "Brian, dinner time."

Still not sure what I was going to do with my new found friend and not wanting to give him up I decided I would put him in a box until after lunch and then figure out what to do.

"I'll be right there," I hollered back and headed for the house.

I was only halfway through the porch door when I saw Gramma waiting for me, "What happened to you?" she asked.

Knowing I was about to be caught red-handed with 'Kermit' and no time to hide him, I did what any seven year old would do – and stuffed him in my pants pocket. You have to understand that pants were much baggier back then and there was lots of room for him not to get squished.

"What... why?" I quickly asked back hoping she had not noticed the frog.

Pointing toward the shaving mirror just inside the door she replied, "Take a look."

The mirror was set for Grampa and Uncle Paul so I had to stand on a little stool to catch my reflection. Looking back at me was this dust-covered face with a dark ring around my mouth and nose surrounding the spots that I had wiped clean. Oh-Oh, I had been busted.

I lowered my head and weakly mumbled: "I, uh, stood too close to the road when Mr. Johnston drove by."

I could feel her eyes searching up and down my shirt sleeves looking for signs of dirt or goobers. She gave both my shirt and pants a brush with her hand - thankfully not on the side where Mr. Frog was stashed – and of course, little clouds of dust puffed out.

"Give me your clothes," she sighed, "I have a load soaking so I might as well wash them as well."

Well now I'm in a pickle – do I fess up and tell her I have a frog in my pocket or bluff my way through and hope the frog sneaks away?

She stretched out her hand and a little less patiently says, "Come on, give them to me."

What could I do, I gave them to her and quietly watched as she tossed them in the soaking tub.

As I'm putting on my clean clothes Gramma heads for the kitchen, grabbed the dipper and filled it full of water from the warmer on the stove and carefully poured it into the washbasin below the mirror. "OK, wash your face, don't forget to clean your ears, we will wash your hair later, and then go eat your lunch, it is getting cold."

Pleased that my deception had not been discovered I sat quietly at the table as I slurped down the homemade chicken soup, occasionally dipping in a slice of yesterday's fresh-baked bread.

I kept glancing out the front window so as not to miss Paul should he come home. A couple of sharp barks from Skipper alerted me that something was happening and I saw him running up the driveway barking as he went. Finally, Uncle Paul's truck came into view. I quickly downed the last couple of spoonfuls of soup and sprang for the door.

"It only takes one person to brighten someone's day!"

Time to Ride

I just got through the door as Uncle Paul drove by, giving me a quick wave as he did and went directly to his workshop. I ran after him and arrived there just as he was getting out of the truck. "Hi, Uncle Paul, where have you been?" I asked.

He just smiled and said, "I'm glad you are here, I could use your help." He walked around to the back of his truck and lowered the tailgate. I tried to see what he had in there but he was standing just in the right spot and the only thing I could see looked like some kind of wheel. He handed me a small cardboard box and said, "Take this over to where the anvil is." Anxious to see what else he had I quickly did as he said and rushed back to the truck.

He promptly handed me a big spoked wheel, "Put this over there with the box."

"What's this for?" I couldn't help asking. He just grinned and pointed towards the shop. I leaned the wheel up against the anvil and when I turned back around towards the truck Uncle Paul was right behind me carrying another wheel and a frame.

Now I had seen a bicycle before, the kids in town would ride them to school, but I had never ridden one and had definitely never seen one in pieces like this before – the tires were flat, the dark red paint was peeling off the frame and some of the parts were covered in rust.

"Is this a bike, who is it for?" I questioned.

"Yep it's a bicycle," he responded, "and it's yours."

I must have looked less than thrilled because I heard Paul say, "I know it doesn't look like much now but we will have it looking just fine by supper time."

Up to this point my 'put things together' experience had been limited to playing with my Meccano and building block sets. "Uhh...we," I asked?

Uncle Paul smiled, "Yup when a person runs a piece of equipment he needs to know how it works, how to care for it and how to fix it when it's broke."

And with that, the learning began. Over the rest of the afternoon, Paul helped me take everything apart and put it back again. We fixed the tires, scraped and brushed the rust, oiled the chain and sprockets and assembled the pedals. Paul then turned the bike upside down and rested the handlebars and seat on the ground. Then he put the front wheel in place and spun it to see if it would run without wobbling. It did have a slight wobble and Paul explained that it meant the wheel was slightly bent and out of alignment. It could be fixed by slowly tightening or loosening the spokes to pull them back into alignment. Five minutes later the tire was running smooth and true. He handed me the wrench and had me do the same thing to the back wheel.

I was beginning to get excited – we were just about done. The last things to do were put on the chain and adjust the back wheel so the chain was 'taunt' but not tight. Paul showed me what that meant. If the chain was too tight it might break if any pressure was put on it

Newer, but similar to mine

and if the chain was too loose it could come off while you were riding. So before you tightened the wheel down you had to move it forward or backward until it was, neither too loose, nor too tight but, just right – taunt.

Finally! Everything was assembled, tightened and tested. Paul turned it upright and asked, "Well, what do think?"

As I proudly looked it over from front to back I realized Paul had been right. "I think it looks terrific!" I exclaimed. "Is it ready to ride?"

With a big grin, Paul replied, "You bet, but I'll try it out first just to make sure everything works like it should."

With that Uncle Paul threw his leg over the bar, put his foot on the pedal and took off across the yard – wobbling at first until he gained his balance. He took a couple of slow trips around the yard and once he had regained his bike riding confidence he took off up the driveway. I ran back towards the house to where I could see him turn around at the highway.

He paused for a moment, waiting for Skipper to get out of his way, put his foot on the pedal and started back down the driveway. He peddled faster and faster and when he went by me I actually heard a 'whoosh'. By the time he slowed down, he was almost at the chicken coop. Satisfied that everything was working the way it should he rode back over to me - "OK, it's your turn," he said.

"Uhh...Uncle Paul, remember I have never ridden a bike before and I'm not sure what I am supposed to do or even how to get on."

Paul chuckled, "Oh yeah, I forgot about that – here let me show you."

With that, he reached down and grabbed the front peddle and moved it to the 10 o'clock position, "You will gain enough speed by the time the pedal reaches the bottom to keep your balance if you start with it here."

He then moved the pedals so they were in the 3 and 9 o'clock positions - "If you want to slow down or just coast for a bit – stop peddling with your pedals just about here. That way it is easy to start peddling again or if you push down on the back pedal that puts the brake on."

He looked at me to make sure I understood. I nodded that I did. "Good. One final thing - hold onto the handlebars with both hands to help with your balance. When you want to turn, don't do it like you do with the steering wheel in a car, or you will crash, just lean slightly in the direction you want to go and turn the handlebars just a little bit." Paul demonstrated it a couple of times until he was convinced that I got it.

Then he moved to the other side of the bike, grabbed the handlebars with one hand and the crossbar with the other. "Ok young fella, I'll hold it steady until you get aboard."

I cautiously took hold of the handlebars, placed my foot squarely on the pedal and nervously swung my leg over the seat and settled down into riding position. There was only one thing wrong. "Uhh…Uncle Paul, I can't reach the pedals," I mumbled.

Paul looked down at my foot dangling high above the pedal on his side. He slyly smiled, "I guess you are a little shorter than me – I'll lower the seat for you."

I hopped off and held the bike while he got his wrench and lowered the seat to the lowest setting. Signaling me to give it a try, I once more mounted my mighty steed, much smoother the second time I must admit and settled back into the seat. "How's that," he asked?

"Much better" I replied. I can just reach the lower pedal where it is right now but I think when it is at the bottom I'm going to have a little trouble."

"Hmmm," Paul's brow furrowed as he seemed puzzled as

what to do next. "Let me think about this for a moment." Leaving me holding the bike he headed for his workshop to figure out a solution.

This is probably a good time to tell you about just how big this bicycle was. My bike tires were 70 cm (28 in) – almost 50% taller than a BMX wheel. Now considering an average 8-year-old only stands 120 cm (48") tall, by the time you add in the bike frame, the handlebars were about the height of my shoulders. At that time I didn't care how big it was – it was my bike and as long as I could reach the pedals I was going to learn how to ride it!

Paul returned from the shop, carrying an old feed sack, a hunk of leather and some binder twine. "Let's try this," he says. He loosened the seat and took it completely off the bike. Then he wrapped the feed sack around the crossbar and over the hole where the seat was. Next, he wrapped the piece of leather around the feed sack and then tied it in place with the binder twine. Surveying his work he grinned and said, "I know it's not pretty but if it works I'll fix it up later."

Without the seat being in the way I found it was much easier getting on this time. The feed sack and leather wrapping provided a good cushion from the metal bar and, best of all, my feet could now reach both pedals – not the ground – but both petals. Paul looked down and saw my feet still dangling, "That is as low as I can get it. Guess you are going to have to grow some this summer – are you ready to give it a go?"

By now my grin was so big I couldn't even talk so I just nodded my approval as he took up a position beside me where he could hang onto the frame just about where the seat used to be.

At that time we had a teardrop-shaped driveway that went around the house and front yard and he explained to me how he was going to go around the driveway with me until I got the feel of pedaling, steering and keeping my balance. After a slow, hesitant, wobbly start he encouraged me, "You are doing great – remember the faster you go the easier it is to keep your balance but harder to turn – go faster on the straight parts and slow down for the corners, not too slow or you will fall over."

By the time we made the second loop Paul was into a full jog and barely hanging on. As we went by our starting point he gave me a little push, let go and said, "Keep pedaling!"

Now either Uncle Paul was a great teacher or I was a quick learner because now I was a bike rider! By the 4th or 5th time around the yard my speed had doubled – still had a little trouble on the corners but loved those straightaways. As I approached Paul I heard him loudly ask, "You think you got it now?"

"I think so," I hollered back, "but..." - by this time I was passed him and had to make one more lap around the house. This time I slowed down as I approached him, "but I don't know how to stop," I pleaded. Paul laughed and reached out and grabbed the bike as I went by and held on until I got stopped. "Guess we should have covered that a little sooner," he said, still smiling.

He proceeded to show me two ways of how I could stop. First, step on the brake (remember there were no hand brakes at that time) until you were almost stopped, take your other foot off the pedal, move it out to the side, and, while still holding onto the handlebars, lean over until your foot hit the ground and stopped your movement and then gently lower the bike to the ground.

Or – and I liked this one much better – just before you stop, keep your foot on the pedal and dismount just like you were riding a horse. But, he cautioned, wait until your balance is a little better because if you don't do it quite right you are probably going to crash and hurt yourself or bang up your bike.

Now, I wasn't worried about me too much but I already loved that bike! It wasn't new and it wasn't fancy but to me, it was just about the most wonderful thing I had ever seen and I wasn't going to take any chances of smacking it up!

Paul made me practice a few times and once he was satisfied I had it figured out said, "Ok, you are on your own. It just about supper time to I'm going to go wash up."

He was almost at the door when it occurred to me that in my excitement I had forgotten something, "Uncle Paul," I hollered.

He looked back towards me, "Yes."

"Thank-you Uncle Paul, Thank-you, this is the best present ever!"

A big grin spread across his face, "You are welcome, my boy, now go have fun."

I had made about another dozen or so trips around the yard when I spotted Linda standing at the front door. "Look at me," I gushed as I went whooshing by, "I'm flying!" By now I was feeling pretty full of myself and tore around the yard as fast as I dared. Before I got to her this time she shouted out, "It's supper time, you are supposed to come in now."

"Ok, just one more time around the yard," I shouted back. As I turned the last corner I could see her still standing at the door. This surprised me because normally she would have gone back inside by now – maybe she was amazed at how good a rider I was already I thought to myself, confidently smiling.

She stood there patiently waiting until I got off my bike, leaned it up against the spruce tree and had almost made it to the front door before she spoke, "Boy, are you in big trouble."

That's when I saw it – the glint in her eyes and a devilish grin – you know, that look, the one where your sibling knows you are in trouble and they are not – yeah, that one. "Whaaat," I stammered, "What did I do, I have been outside all day?"

Linda flashed the look again and as she turned to go back inside she gloatingly said, "Oh, I don't know – Gramma said something about a frog. Do you know anything about a frog?"

Oh, oh, the frog! Did I forget about the frog – I had forgotten about the frog. Busted! There was only one thing to do – fess up and beg for mercy – with that I opened the door and stepped through.

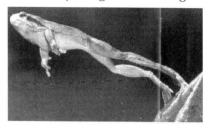

"When someone gives you a present or helps you, always say 'Thank you' – who knows, they might even do it again"

Frog and the Washing Machine

Wouldn't you know it – just as I stepped through the door I caught Gramma on her way back from putting supper on the table and she was staring right through me! The wrinkles on her forehead were so deep they cast shadows over her squinted eyes that were shooting lightning bolts right through me. Owww! Owww! – I could almost feel the pain as they burned into my skin. I started to stammer, "I'm…I'm sorry Gramma," but she stopped me cold in my tracks - "Wash up and go eat your supper."

I quickly did as I was told and joined the rest of them at the dinner table. I glanced over at Grampa and Uncle Paul but they had their heads down and were studying their plates as if they had never seen moose meat and mashed potatoes before. Only Linda would look at me – still with that devilish little smile – she was enjoying this.

That was the quietest meal I think we ever ate. Nobody said a word, not even Linda – and that was a big deal for her! This was worse than getting scolded or punished – not that it happened very often to me, but I could feel that this time I had really messed up somehow. Couldn't quite figure it though – this was not the first time I had left something in my pockets, true it never had been a frog, but Gramma had always checked my pockets and removed any bits of hidden treasure. It was normally followed up with a finger-wagging, a slight scolding and a promise from me never to do it again – but this time was different.

I snuck a glance toward Gramma to see if she had mellowed down over supper but caught her looking right at me. BAM, another lightning bolt almost blinded me.

As I got closer and closer to finishing my supper I started eating slower and slower. I knew that as soon as I finished I was on the firing line. Grampa and Paul had already finished, had pulled their chairs back from the table and were doing their best to look interested in some far off part of the living room. Not Linda though – she just kept staring at me and grinning that evil grin – boy, was I going to get her later! I had barely gotten that last bite into my mouth when Gramma looked at me – brow furrowed, eyes squinted, lips pursed and finally spoke – she didn't yell or get excited – just a low even-tempered, you had better pay attention, tone.

"I'm not even going to ask why there was a frog in your pocket, I can figure that out, but why didn't you take it out when you gave your pants to me?"

I opened my mouth to give her my best, "I'm sorry," but she held up her 'shushing' finger and wagged it at me.

She continued, "I have told you before about leaving stuff in your pockets. I can understand forgetting about a small toy or a piece of string but a FROG!"

Gramma paused a moment to let it sink in and when she had determined that I seeing the seriousness of the situation she went on, "Because I was still putting dinner on the table I didn't check your pockets this time and just threw your pants in with the rest of the wash that was soaking. Now maybe because the frog was small it stayed in your pocket through the wash. Can you guess what happens when a FROG goes through the wringer?"

It's amazing what you notice when you are paying full attention and waiting for the hammer to drop – Gramma had leaned forward, the 'shushing' finger was pointed right at me, her voice was slightly louder, definitely more excited and it seemed to have even more of an English accent than usual. Not sure if I was supposed to answer or not, I just waited to see what was going to happen next.

Now, this seems to be a good time to break into the story and tell you what a big job doing laundry was back then. Remember, we had no electricity and no running water. You couldn't just open the lid, throw in the clothes, turn a dial and have almost everything done for you.

Doing laundry was hard work and a full day's job. First Grampa would have to go to the dugout – about 100 metres away – and get maybe 14 or 15 pails of water.

Some of them would be put on top of the woodstove until the water was warm. I'm sure it never got really hot because that would have taken too long.

It was then poured into the washing machine. As the same water was used for all the laundry, the clothes had to be separated and done in a set order – whites and delicates first, followed by sleepwear, dress clothes and dirty work/play clothes last. If any of them had stains, mud or grease on them they were hand scrubbed, with a scrubbing board, before they went into the wash.

The washing machine was in the back porch and had a gasoline engine. So that we wouldn't get overcome by the gas fumes, a rubber hose was attached to the exhaust pipe and fed through a hole in the wall to the outside. Once Gramma had the first load ready to wash she would start the engine which would turn the agitator – you know that tall spindle thing with blades on it – and let the clothes wash for about 5 minutes.

The next step was to take the clothes out of the soapy water and run them through the wringer, one at a time. That would squeeze most of the soapy water back into the washing machine. The clothes then dropped down into a big grey galvanized tub, (the same one we took our baths in on Saturday night), filled with clean rinsing water.

Once the clothes had been hand rinsed they were put through the wringer again – this time put into a basket that could be carried. More water that had been heating on the stove would be added to the tub and the next load would be put in to soak.

We did not use a separate ringer

Gramma would take the basket out to the clotheslines; I think there were two of them that ran from trees close to the crystal palace to other trees about 7 metres away. Using wooden clothes pegs she would carefully hang each item on the line. Then it was back inside to start the process all over again – sometimes four or five times depending on what was being washed that day.

Hopefully wash day was a warm sunny day with a stiff breeze. Then the lighter clothes and bedsheets would dry in less than thirty minutes and heavier work clothes would maybe take an hour or two – unless a rain shower appeared. Then you had to run out and quickly take all the clothes down, wait for the shower to pass and then rehang them all again.

Winter was another story – if you left the clothes on the line for more than half an hour they would become frozen solid like a sheet of ice. They would be taken inside and hungover chairs, doorknobs, coat hooks – anywhere they could hang to finish drying.

Ok, back to the story – as I sat there waiting for Gramma to speak it occurred to me that I had never really wondered about how the washing was done. Whenever Gramma decided it was time to change clothes the dirty ones disappeared and clean ones appeared. I was getting a funny feeling that I was about to get a whole new understanding about washing clothes.

"Well do you?"

Even though I was still a little kid I was smart enough to know this was not a good time to say anything so I just meekly shook my head.

"Have you ever dropped an egg on the ground?" she asked.

I nodded, yes, I had.

"And what did it do," she continued, "did it go 'splat' with egg all over the place?"

Again I nodded in agreement.

"Well that is what happens when you put a frog through the wringer – it goes 'splat' all over the place!"

I quickly glanced over at Uncle Paul and Grampa. Both of them had their heads turned away from the table and I could tell they were desperately trying not to laugh. Linda, on the other hand, was still grinning big time – she was enjoying this way too much!

From past experiences, limited experiences mind you; I knew there was only one thing to do. I lowered my eyes towards my plate and sheepishly said, "I'm sorry Gramma, it won't happen again."

With that, her face softened and she leaned back in her chair. She gave a soft sigh and said, "Lucky for you, it was the last load, and a small frog, so no real damage was done."

Figuring I was now off the hook I pushed away from the table, planning to head outside and do some more bike riding when I heard, "BUT".

Ooh! Ooh! This wasn't good – I didn't like 'buts', they were always trouble.

"I have a chore for you to do. Remember this is also a bath night. Normally Grampa gets the water BUT I think you could use a little time to reflect on what you did. So we are going to give Grampa the night off and you are going to haul the bathwater – about 6-7 pails should do it."

I knew I wasn't big enough to carry a full pail so that was going to be a lot of trips back and forth to the dugout. I looked over at Grampa hoping he might help me out but he just cocked his head to the side and slightly grinned, as if to remind me of what he had once said, "Gramma doesn't put her foot down very often, but when she does - it stays down!"

It seemed to take forever – I don't know how many trips I had to make back and forth but I do remember how tuckered out I was by the time Gramma put her hand gently on my shoulder and said, "That's enough water, I think you have learned your lesson. It will be about half an hour until the water is ready, so go outside and ride your new bike."

As I walked across the yard I thought to myself, "What a day! I caught a frog, got a new bike, learned how to ride a bike and also learned –

"If you mess up – be very, very sorry and hope for some sympathy" and "Never, ever leave a frog in your pocket."

Bikes Don't Float

It was a couple of weeks after I had gotten my bike. We had just finished our soup and sandwiches, when Uncle Paul announced, "The tractor was running a little rough this morning so I think I'll go work on it and see if I can figure out what is wrong."

Grampa followed Paul over to the door, put on his hat and said, "Well I think I will go and get the mail now," and headed out the door. Every week, when the weather was nice, Grampa would walk down to the community store, about 3 km away, to collect the mail and maybe visit a bit.

As Gramma gathered up the dishes from the table she looked over at Linda and me, "It is a nice day out there, why don't the two of you go and visit Aunt Barbara for a while?"

Whether she thought Barb would like some company or whether she just wanted some quiet time – I personally think that after having Linda home from school for a couple of weeks now, she was such a chatterbox, always singing and playing make-believe with her dolls, that Gramma just wanted some quiet time!

It didn't matter, Linda always loved visiting with Aunt Barbara and, if he wasn't too busy, Uncle Stan would show or talk to me about different things than what I had learned from Uncle Paul.

Sensing an opportunity to show off my newly acquired riding skills I asked, "Is it OK if I take my bike?"

Gramma replied, "If you want to but NO riding on the highway, you need more practice yet - stay between the trees and the ditch and," her voice becoming a little sterner, "Don't leave your sister behind, you wait for her – there are still bears roaming around."

Bears! We hadn't seen a bear in almost a month but I wasn't about to argue – I was still stinging over the scolding I had received a few days earlier about the frog and I wasn't going to take any chances getting her angry again. "Ok," I sighed, "I will wait for her."

Gramma smiled, "Good – take Skipper with you, he will know if there is a bear around before you do." Which, after my experiences the previous year, I was quite OK with it.

Although Stan's farm was only about 300m away it was slightly uphill most of the way. It wasn't much of a path, just a haphazard journey through the weeds that we had knocked down on our previous visits. It was too rough to ride on – especially at the pace Linda was moving. She was forever stopping to smell a flower, watch a ladybug or catch a butterfly – and people wonder where I learned my patience from! It was tough pushing that heavy bike through the loose dirt and by the time we reached Stan and Barb's I was huffing and puffing. I was done with walking – it was time to RIDE!

As soon as we got to the approach off the highway into their yard, Bowser – their yellowish, medium-sized Heinz 57 dog – had heard us coming and was bounding out to meet us, tail wagging and barking 'hello' the whole way. Linda took off running and skipping towards the house with Bowser, still barking, running beside her, trying to get her attention.

I stood beside my bike for a moment, to catch my breath, and surveyed the yard. A few metres in front of me the road turned into a really nice sized slightly oval driveway. The house was on one side, a new lawn in the middle and the dugout, about 3-4 metres from the road, on the other side. At the other end, a small road continued on to the granaries and shop outback.

I plotted my plan of attack – I figured I would go straight down passed the dugout and then make the turn towards the house and then down the straightaway by the house. By then I should have built up some good speed and should anybody be watching surely they would marvel what a good rider I was already.

Ok, foot on the pedal, leg over the bar, and I was off. I quickly discovered that Stan had more gravel on his driveway than we did and that made the front tire bounce around some. I decided it might be a good idea to go a little slow the first time around until I got used to it – and to determine if there might be any ruts hiding under the gravel that I should be aware of. I had already learned about ruts – if you are not paying attention and your tire catches one you could be in for a good spill – happened to me a couple of times in the past few days. A mouth full of dirt and a skinned knuckle or two was bad enough but I had been warned about gravel. It could give you quite a road rash real quick.

The first time around the oval, everything going good, no ruts to worry about and if I held onto the handlebars a little tighter I could almost stop the front wheel from wobbling. I also found out that when I rode a little faster the bike was easier to control. You know what that meant – the second time around was faster than the first and by the third time my little legs were pumping just as hard as they could – I was flying!

I was starting to feel pretty full of myself and sure hoped somebody was watching me tear around the driveway. Well, somebody was, but it was not who I was expecting. On my fourth pass by the house, just a running and barking came Bowser. And he started chasing me around the driveway.

I don't know if Bowser had ever seen a bicycle before and I

wasn't sure if he thought it was something he should attack or if he just wanted to play but when he got up beside me he started lunging at my pant leg trying to get a hold of it. Whatever he was trying to do I didn't want any part of it so as soon as I hit the straightaway I peddled as hard as I could hoping to outrun him.

Unfortunately for me, Bowser was smarter than he looked. He made a quick left turn and ran across the lawn to meet me on the other side. This time he started running before I went by him and caught me just as I slowed down a little for the corner. Once, twice, three times he lunged at my pant leg, finally sinking his teeth into them on the last try. He snapped his head back and pulled my foot completely off the pedal. I started shaking my leg as hard as I could, while still maintaining my balance, to try and break loose from his grip.

Maybe because he thought he had won and let go or maybe it was because my pant leg, which had been rolled up, was now unraveling and he just lost his grip it didn't matter – I was free again. I put my foot back on the pedal figuring I would ride around to the house and take a breather, and let Bowser quiet down some before I tried again. The pedals had only gone around 2 or 3 times when I felt another tug on my pant leg. Just as I looked down I saw the cuff of my pants disappear between the sprocket and the chain. As the sprocket went around it pulled my pant leg with it and that pulled my foot off the pedal which pulled me forward on the crossbar and had me leaning over the handlebars – desperately trying to stay upright and not crash.

Now might be a good time to explain a couple of things. One – we didn't have form-fitting jeans back then. Our pants tended to be a little baggier and the cuffs would flop around quite a bit. Two – my bicycle did not have a chain guard which meant there was nothing between my pant leg and the chain.

So if your pant leg flopped the right way, at the right time on the upstroke it could get caught on the teeth of the sprocket and held in place by the chain as it was pulled down on to the teeth. As the sprocket continued forward and down it would pull your pant leg along with the chain. This would pull your foot off the pedal and then you were in no man's land – you couldn't pedal and you couldn't put your feet on the ground.

Again, I had already experienced this in the past few days and the results were the same as the ruts – mud and grass in the mouth, scrapes on the hands and a bump on the head.

Uncle Paul had explained to me there was pretty much only one way out. That was to wait until you were just about stopped, put your untangled foot out and then fall over as gently as you could.

Then you could turn the pedals by hand until your pants had gone all way around the sprocket and popped out at the bottom. He then showed me how to roll up that one pant leg so it would stay up and not get caught in the chain again.

Notice the rolled up pant leg

Ok, where was I? There I was, leaning over the handlebars – desperately trying to stay upright and not to crash until I could find a landing spot. Unfortunately as I was looking down, my sudden lurch forward had changed my direction and I was no longer on the driveway but instead was heading straight for the dugout with the water just a metre away.

I glanced right because that was the way I was supposed to

fall, but the small dock they used to get water from the dugout was right there. If I crashed into it I could get seriously hurt. There was nothing left to do but flop over to the left and take my chances.

Just as my front tire went over the edge of the dugout over I went. I bounced off the ground; the bike did too – the back end swung around and went over the edge as well. Luckily for me, that was the shallow end of the dugout and the grade wasn't very steep. Still, with nothing to hold it back except me, the bike started to slip into the water – dragging me along with it.

"HELP, HELP!" I hollered. By now I was up to my knees in the water and still slowly sliding forward. "HELP, HELP," I hollered again sure hoping somebody other than Bowser was going to help me. I was in the middle of debating whether I could get my shoes and pants off before the bike pulled me under when I heard, "HOLD ON," and one big friendly hand grabbed me and the other grabbed my bike and pulled us to safety. Uncle Stan lifted up the bike and spun the wheel around until my pants became free. He looked me over, "You alright?"

I checked myself over and except some wet pants and a grass stain on my shirt, I seemed to be undamaged. "Yep," I answered, "You got here just in time – thanks for pulling me out Uncle Stan."

"I was watching you ride, you were going pretty fast until Bowser got a hold of you," He gave a little chuckle and said, "Why don't you take a break for a little bit? I bet your Auntie has got some fresh baked cookies in the house."

You didn't have to tell me twice – I liked Aunt Barbara's cookies!

Afterwards Bowser and I came to an understanding – if I rode around the yard slow like until he got used to me, he wouldn't chase me. The couple of times I thought he might chase me I quickly stopped riding, waited for him to get bored and go back to his kennel. I wasn't taking any chances – once in the dugout was enough for me!

"Always make peace with the dog – he might not understand what you are up to."

Ok, here are two stories in one that set up a third – about Cowboys and a bike and how they don't always go together"

Riding or Roping – What to do?

That summer was just about over as I stood on the back porch step for a few moments, pondering on what I should do first – ride my bike or twirl my lasso.

I had spent a lot of time riding my bike over the last two summers and had gotten pretty good on it – including a couple of simple tricks. The past couple of months I had been practicing riding with no hands which, let me tell you, is not all that easy on gravel or dirt roads. Lumps of dirt and ruts would catch the front wheel and throw you off balance real quick – I had more than a few spills the first few days.

Luckily I had gotten no more than a few scrapes and bruises for my efforts. I was also smart enough to practice on the side road that went by our place – it was straight, reasonably smooth and of most importance, out of the view of Gramma – I'd have gotten the 'Royal what for' if she had caught me doing such a fool thing!

I had also received good advice from one of the older community boys, the one who talked me into this 'fool thing' in the first place. "Start with learning how to ride first with one hand and then the other. Figure out what speed you should go – too slow and the slightest bump will throw you off balance – too fast and you won't be able to gain control before you go over. When you feel you are ready, lift your hands slowly off the handlebars but only a couple of inches at first because the bike is going to wobble more than you are used to. Next, sit up straight; it is much easier to keep your balance that way. One more thing – tighten the nut on the handlebars – it will make it harder to steer but the front wheel won't wobble so much."

It didn't take more than a couple of mouthfuls of dirt and gravel rash on my hands to learn that these were true words of wisdom and so I followed what he had said. I hadn't crashed in almost three days now and was feeling so good about myself that I had started riding around the yard even navigating shallow turns here and there.

But – I was also enjoying playing with my lasso.

Earlier that summer, one morning at breakfast, Uncle Paul asked me, "You want to be a real cowboy don't you?"

Of course, I did - it was every young boy's dream to be a real cowboy (or gunfighter). I nodded enthusiastically and waited for him to continue.

"Well, a real cowboy needs a good rope if he is going to round up them there cows and trail drive them to market, doesn't he?" It didn't make any difference to me that we didn't have any cows, maybe someday we might and I wanted to be ready, "You are right Uncle Paul, if I am going to be a real cowboy I need a lasso."

"All right my boy; let's go make you a lasso." With that, he got up and signaled me to follow him. We went over to his shop where he took a large roll of rope down from the wall. He laid one end on the ground and walked off about 5 paces (5 metres), "I think that will long enough to start with, when your hands get a little bigger I will make you a longer one. Sound good?"

I didn't really understand what he meant at that point but I figured he knew what he was talking about so I quickly agreed with him, "You bet, Uncle Paul – what do we do now?"

He picked up one end of the rope and began unraveling a few centimetres of it. "We have to make an opening for the other end of the rope to go through – small enough to hold the rope in place while you are twirling it but large enough that it slides easily to snug up around a cow's neck."

With that, he proceeded to show me how to splice (braid) the unraveled strands into the rope to form a nice oblong loop. He then took some tape and wrapped around the spliced part to hold it all in place. He also taped the oblong loop so when it slid up and down the rope it wouldn't fray (destroy, wear out) the fine strands of the rope. Finally, he taped the other end of the rope so it wouldn't come apart and pushed it through the taped up hole to make a loop. "Ok, let's step outside and I'll show you how to hold the rope, make a loop and throw it."

He opened his hand and coiled the rope in it, making 4 medium size loops and then loosely closed his fingers around the rope. He explained that if you made the loops too big they might catch on your saddle or something and if you made them too small they wouldn't come out of your hand easily when you threw the rope and that it would be different for each person, so I would just have to experiment until I found out what worked for me.

Step 2 – He took the throwing loop in his other hand, showed me where to put my fingers and how to shake it gently so it would grow to the size you wanted. Again he stressed – if the loop was too small it wouldn't twirl properly and if it was too big it would be too difficult to control – only practice would determine what the right size was for me.

I was with him so far but I was getting anxious to do some twirlin' and ropin'. I think Uncle Paul noticed because he smiled and said, "Ok cowboy, let's mosey over towards the woodpile and I'll show you how to catch something."

I noticed as we started walking that he was shaking his wrist a little bit and the loop was getting bigger and bigger, then he gave a little flick of his wrist and quickly raised his arm over his head rotating his wrist as his arm went up – and there it was – a great big circle twirling over his head. He looked down at me and grinned, "Did you catch that? Looked easy, didn't it? It will be once you get the hang of it."

He twirled it all the way to the woodpile and when he got just the right distance away he brought his arm back behind his head and then gave a mighty throw. The loop flew through the air towards an axe that was stuck into the chopping block. As the rope settled over the handle he gave a slight jerk of his arm and the noose tightened around the axe handle. I was impressed – and on the first throw too!

After a few more minutes of instruction and demonstrations, Paul decided I was ready to give it a go. Let's just say it didn't go all that well at the beginning – the first time, I moved my arm too fast and the rope couldn't keep up and I promptly smacked myself in the face with it. The next time I got it up in the air but twirled it too slow for the size of noose I had and it fell out of the sky – I had lassoed my own head! After a few more tries I was a twirling expert and ready to do some throwing.

And that didn't go much better than the twirling thing. Paul had replaced the axe with a block of wood because it was a little bigger and would be easier to rope. My first few tries landed about a metre in front of me, behind me, to the left, right and over the wood - if there was a way to miss it, I did it. And finally – there was that one well-timed throw and I had successfully caught my first cow...err...block of wood. It would take another 10 minutes before I could duplicate that sweet smell of success!

So I had been practicing my twirling and throwing for a few weeks now and had improved immensely. I had graduated from blocks of wood to tree stumps, fence posts, farm equipment – if I could get a rope on it, it was caught. I'll tell you, Linda and Skipper were pretty nervous around me for a while and if they saw me with the rope they wouldn't come anywhere near me.

So here I was, wasting the morning away trying to decide what was I going to do -Riding or Roping – and then it struck me – I could do both!

I was about to learn the meaning of an old saying –

"The best of plans often don't work out the way they were intended"

A Bike Ain't No Horse

It seemed like a great idea – at the time! I could pretend my bike was a horse and then I could be a real cowboy.

I gathered up my rope, hopped on my bike and headed for the side road – I was smart enough to know that if I was going to get into trouble for riding with no hands, I would be in double-trouble for trying to ride and rope at the same time.

Once I got to the side road, and out of sight of the house, I stopped and adjusted my hold on the rope. I let out just enough rope to make a medium-sized loop and put it into one set of fingers. The rest I gathered into the other hand with about a metre or so of loose rope in between – I figured that would give me enough to twirl just above my head without any danger of being caught in the pedals or front wheel.

I looked down the side road, it had a slight slope for about 200 metres and then it gently dipped into the valley beyond, it looked ok and there were no cars coming. I put my hands on the handlebar, took a deep breath, swung my leg over the bar and started peddling. As I gained speed I gently let go of the handlebar with one hand. Satisfied I had my balance I raised my arm above my head and started twirling.

WHOA! A violent bobble of the front wheel and a vision of a painful crash brought my arm quickly down to grab the handlebar to get the bike back under control. I was too close to the top of the hill to try again so I turned the bike around and headed back to my starting point. Once there I sat in the grass and waited for my heart to stop pounding – Whew! That had been a close one – but I wasn't ready to give up yet.

Over the next couple of hours and a few more near spills I slowly learned a few things:

I couldn't pedal and twirl at the same time (not yet anyway) because it was too difficult to keep one's balance. The trick was to get up enough speed and then coast.

Starting the twirl over my head caused too much side to side motion and made it difficult to keep my balance. It was much easier to start the twirl to the side while my hand was just above waist level and then slowly lifted my hand above my head, keeping my arm still as I could and just using my wrist to twirl the rope.

Once I got the rope twirling I could let go of the bars with my other hand and bring it in closer to my body. This allowed me to sit up straighter, which gave me better balance and allowed me to slowly pedal (downhill only) to keep my speed up and therefore giving me a longer ride.

I also figured out that, while twirling, if I brought my arm back behind my head and without too sudden of a move I could actually throw the lasso, forward and slightly to the side, about 2 metres.

After a number of successful throws, and now being an expert, you just know that I need something to rope – Skipper has been watching and he wouldn't come anywhere near me, the fence alongside the road was too far away and so were the overhanging tree branches – what was I going to do?

There was only one thing to do, find something in the yard to rope and take my chances of being caught. Sure enough, Uncle Paul had moved a piece of equipment, a swather I think, that he was getting ready for the harvest and left it right beside the driveway. Wouldn't you know it – there was an iron bar, about head-height, sticking straight up out to the side of it – perfect!

There was only one problem – it was on a direct line of sight from the kitchen window. Before I tried such a 'foolhardy thing' I figured I had better make sure Gramma wasn't doing something in the kitchen.

As soon as I entered the house I gave a quick glance around – Linda was on the day bed, propped up by the pillows, reading a book – Grampa was in his chair, pretending to read, while having a snooze – and Gramma was sitting at the table, mending some of Uncle Paul's pants. She looked up, "Need something," she asked?

"Nope," I answered as I reached down and grabbed the dipper off the water barrel, "Just came in for a drink. Where is Uncle Paul?"

"He is at the neighbours helping fix something, should be home soon," she answered and then went back to her sewing.

I took a quick slurp of the water and put the dipper back on the lid of the barrel, "Ok," I replied. Satisfied that now was as good time as any to not get caught I hurried back outside, grabbed my bike and rode up to the start of the driveway.

I calculated that I could get up enough speed by the time I reached the house to enable me to coast to the swather, getting in 3 or 4 twirls before I got there and be in perfect position for a throw as I went by.

Rope ready, I peddled down the driveway gaining speed. As I passed the house I started my sideways twirl, slowly lifted my hand above my head, let go of the handlebar with my other hand pulling it in front of me, sat up for balance and stared at my target.

What I felt like!

As soon as I got within what I thought was the right distance I gave a short flick of my arm and wrist and the loop went swirling towards my cow...ahh...target and floated down over the top just as it was intended to.

Now there is that moment in between the amazement that the plan actually worked, the sense of pride that you accomplished your goal and the sudden realization that maybe you hadn't thought the plan all the way through!

It was at this moment that I discovered, that in my hurry not to get caught, I did not have a plan of action should I actually succeed in roping the iron bar. It had not occurred to me that a bike does not stop like a horse does when you rope something. It had not occurred to me that if the bike was not going to stop I maybe should let go of the rope.

It was in that moment, right after I watched the rope settled over the peg as I went by it and thinking, "Wow, I did it," that I saw the rope draw taunt and felt a tug on the rope still wrapped around my other hand.

Before I could yell, "Whoa Horse," not that it would have done any good anyways, or step on the brake, my steed was going in one direction and I was flying off backwards in the other direction landing flat on my back with a resounding THUD.

Luckily for me, the ground was reasonably soft and the weeds were tall enough to somewhat cushion my fall, but still, it was enough to knock the wind out of me. As I lay there catching my breath I wiggled my fingers and toes, everything worked and nothing but my pride was hurt so I guessed I was OK. I turned my head and glanced towards the house – I felt a great sense of relief when I saw no one had witnessed my epic oops!

I gathered up my rope and decided I had done enough riding for the time being, pushed my bike back to the ice house. Although I couldn't help but feel a great deal of satisfaction in accomplishing my goal I was also smart enough to figure out that my bike wasn't a horse and a swather wasn't a steer and that my ridin' and ropin' days were done – well at least for a little while anyways.

And the other thing I learned –

"Always take a little extra time to figure out what to do if your plan doesn't work out the way you expected – have a plan 'B'"

Don't Make the Sista' Mad

On long winter nights there was not a whole lot that Linda and I could do. It was too dark by the time we got home from school to play outside. Plus, we were already cold - it was now an hour ride each way on the bus to our new school in Spirit River and that bus didn't have much heat – there were many days we had to scrape the ice off the windows just so we could see whose stop we were at.

So we spent most of our evenings either reading, playing cards or board games. This particular evening we had settled on a card game called 'War'. Have you ever played it? It is a pretty simple game – no skill required just a lot of luck. Linda liked it because it was a game she frequently won. It goes something like this;

Each player gets 26 cards. You start by both of you turning a card face up in front of you. Whoever has the highest card takes both and adds them to the bottom of their pile. Whenever both of you turn over the same card you yell "War." Each of you then plays 3 cards face down on top of the war card and a fourth card face up. Again, whoever has the highest card takes them all. If you tie in the face-up card you repeat the war challenge. You continue like this until one player has all the cards. They win!

On this particular night, Linda has already won two games and is feeling pretty good about herself. On the third game I was still holding my own, maybe a few cards down, but I was hanging in there – and then she hits a lucky streak – wins 4 war challenges in a row – and every time she wins she gives a little bounce and giggles, "I win, I win!"

I should point out that the day bed, we were sitting cross-legged on, was very narrow so we were almost sitting side by side, slightly angled, but less than a ruler length apart.

So when she leaned forward to pick up her cards we were very, very close which made her taunting even worse. Even by the third war, but

Nice plaid shirts! &Curlers!

especially by the fourth, I was getting a little irritated. I was almost out of cards and not happy about it.

The wins went back and forth for a bit and then, "WAR." I laid down my three cards and turned over my fourth – tied – double WAR! Again, I laid down my three cards and turned over the last card in my hand – it was a Jack. Alright, I thought, I got this; I'm back in the game. And then Linda turns over her fourth card – it was a King.

She started bouncing up and down, "I win, I win, I win again!"

"You little !#$!&," I quietly hissed and gave her a brotherly shove on her shoulders, knocking her face down on the bed. Bouncing right back up, her back almost facing me she turned her head, "That wasn't very nice," she growled.

I reached out to give her another push when she snapped her elbow back and nailed me right in the chompers. "Owww," I hollered and instinctively put my hand over my mouth.

At the same time, Gramma had jumped out of her chair and was halfway across the room, "What did you call her?"

As soon as I glanced in her direction I could see the lightning bolts aimed directly at me. I immediately went into self-preservation mode, shrugging my shoulders, shaking my head and giving a wide-open blank stare as if to say, "What, what did I say?"

By now Gramma was right in front of me; her finger pointed directly at my mouth and angrily repeated, "What did you call her?"

Before I could protest my innocence, again, I heard her say, "My goodness, you are bleeding, don't move I will get a wet cloth."

She returned with a small bowl and a warm wet face cloth. She gently washed the blood off my lips and told me to spit in the bowl so if there was any more blood it wouldn't get on the bedspread. I leaned forward, opened my lips slightly and spit – 'Clink' – what was that? Blood doesn't clink. We all looked in the bowl and there was my front tooth – not a baby front tooth – my adult front tooth – the one that doesn't grow back!

Gramma took me over to the sink and got me to rinse out my mouth and then inspected the damage. Other than a fat lip and a missing tooth everything was fine. She told me to put the cloth in the space between the teeth, bite down and keep it there until the bleeding stopped.

On the way back to the couch Gramma put her hand on my back and softly said, "See what happens when you call someone a bad name. Don't ever let me hear you use that word again, do you understand?" Still not knowing what I had said I meekly nodded that I understood. "Good," she continued, "Now go and read for a while and stay still."

It wasn't until many years later that I found out what I had called Linda. There are 2 meanings to the word I used, the way I meant it –

1. to express annoyance or anger. And

2. The other meaning – which I am not going to tell you, but to my English grandparents, it was a nasty swear word. Because I really did not know what I had said, the strongest curse word I ever dared use for many, many years was 'darn' – nobody seemed to get to upset with that one.

Gramma never punished me. I guess she figured that by having to go to school with a missing tooth and a fat lip and having to explain to everybody how my sister whupped me was punishment enough. I talked with a whistle and a lisp until I was in junior high and a wayward basketball knocked my other front tooth out – then I got a partial plate and could smile again without having to tell a story.

This I learned and practiced –

"Be very careful making the 'Sista' mad and definitely not when you are within elbowing range."

Who Doesn't Like Caramel Ripple?

One day Uncle Paul had to make a trip into Spirit River and he took Linda and me along. At this time a lady named Nellie ran a coffee shop in Gordondale. She had asked Paul to pick up some vanilla ice cream for her while he was in town. While Paul was picking up some parts, he asked Linda and me to get the ice cream - which we were more than happy to do. In those days Ice Cream was a big treat and Paul had promised to take us to get some of that ice cream right after supper. Although we were not used to being left on our own, in town, we bravely, hand in hand, marched down the street to the store.

Everything was going just fine until the lady asked, "What kind of ice cream did you want? I have vanilla, strawberry, chocolate, caramel ripple or blah, blah, blah." Linda didn't hear anything after caramel ripple. That's what she wanted. Now I told her we were supposed to buy vanilla, but do you remember how tough I said she was? Needless to say, we left the store with the caramel ripple.

As our icebox was not big enough to keep the ice cream in, Paul dropped Linda and I off at the farm and delivered the ice cream to the coffee shop. We were so excited we could hardly wait for the afternoon to pass. True to his word, as soon as supper was over Paul announced he was going down to the store. As Linda and I prepared to pile into the truck the unexpected happened. "I'm sorry but you don't get to come this time."

This had never happened before. No ice cream. It was unthinkable! "But...but you promised." And then Paul explained reality to us. By not doing what we agreed to do we had let him down, Nellie down and all her customers down. Caramel ripple might be a good ice cream but it wasn't what she wanted and it really didn't go all that well with blueberry pie.

Paul drove off and left us standing in the yard – shocked and broken-hearted. When he got back all he said was "you were right, it was good ice cream." Talk about cruel and unusual punishment. You know we never did get any of that ice cream. We found out Paul could be really tough when he wanted to be. Now I don't know about Linda but I learned some valuable lessons that day –

"Before you make a decision, form an opinion or make a judgment – look at it first from the other person's point of view" and "If you agree to do something, do what you agreed to."

Who Wants Ice Cream?

Linda and I were still mumbling about how we got robbed in the caramel ripple caper when Aunt Barb showed up at the house a couple of weeks later carrying a bucket with a handle under one arm and asked, "Who would like some ice cream?"

Well, that immediately got our attention and two voices in unison excitedly shouted, "I do, I do!"

We followed Barb over to the table and almost butting heads we peered into the bucket - it appeared to be empty except for this metal tube thing and some blades around the sides of it. "Where's the ice cream?" we quizzed.

Barb grinned, "We have to make it first."

"What? You can do that?" We had never heard of such a thing, "How?"

"First we need to get all the ingredients together. I went over to the Johnsons earlier and got a jar of cream but we still need some sugar and condensed milk. Gramma, do you have any vanilla to give it some flavour?"

As Gramma went to get the rest of the ingredients Barb motioned me to follow her. "We also need ice to cool it down to make ice cream." Grabbing a hatchet and a pail as we went through the porch, we headed over to the ice house. There we broke off three decent sized pieces and put them in the pail. Back in the porch she took a hammer and broke the ice into much smaller pieces. "Ok, that is good for now, let's go back into the house and see how Linda and Gramma are doing."

Gramma had made up a large saucepan of milk, added in a drop or two of vanilla seasoning and Linda was stirring the sugar into the liquid. Barb opened her jar of cream and got Linda to stir that in as well.

Barb instructed me to go get the ice and bring the hammer as well. By the time I got back, she had a large tea towel spread out on the floor. "Ok, empty some of the ice onto the tea cloth." Once I did that she wrapped the tea cloth around the ice and holding the bundle tight at one end told me to smash the ice into little bits. The next steps were to add the mixture into the metal container in the bucket, seal it tight and finally pour the crushed ice all around it.

Barb grabbed hold of the handle and said, "Now we crank." It was tough going at first – the metal container didn't move, it was the blades that went round and round moving the ice around the container – this is what made it cold. Some of the ice pieces were still a little big and they wouldn't move easily until they broke down into smaller pieces.

Barb cranked for a few moments until it got easier and then looked at me, "Your turn."

I cranked until my arm got tired and then switched to the other hand. I cranked and cranked some more until that arm got tired and then I switched back to the first hand.

Finally, I got tired and turned to Linda, "Your turn," and passed the handle over to her. She cranked for a little while, but being smaller than and not as strong as me, she couldn't crank fast enough to keep the ice moving so I took over again. Finally, I told Barb, who was visiting with Gramma, "I need a rest. How long is this supposed to take?"

"Oh, a little while yet, let me take over for a bit." She cranked for five minutes or so and finally declared, "Ok, let's have a look." She took the top off the container and we all peered inside – nope it was still liquid. Noticing that the ice was turning to slush she got me to smash up another chunk, into smaller pieces this time and pour them into the bucket. Barb continued cranking until she got tired and again turned it over to me.

I couldn't help but ask again, "how long does this normally take?"

She gave me a little quizzical look and said, "I don't really know – I have never made ice cream before but the people who loaned me the bucket said it should take about a half-hour to forty-five minutes – so we aren't there yet."

This was not what I wanted to hear but it was too early to give up so – I cranked and cranked and then cranked some more. Linda cranked. Barbara cranked. Every once in awhile we would check – maybe it was getting thicker – hard to tell. We added more ice and continued to crank. We cranked until our arms felt like they were going to fall off.

Finally, after what seemed forever Barb shook her head, "I'm not sure why but I don't think this is working – maybe we should just eat what we have."

She sure wasn't getting any argument from me. I wasn't even sure I could lift a spoon by this point. Barb took the top off the machine and poured, not scooped, poured our efforts into a bowl – it looked like ice cream that had been sitting in a warm room for an hour – some texture, but mainly mush. Grampa took one look and declared that 'nope' he was good. Gramma said the same.

I think Gramma felt a little sorry for us because she went and got some of the berries she had picked the day before and added them to our 'ice cream'. Actually, it didn't taste too bad, the berries helped but later on Linda and I agreed that it was way too much work for such a small reward – we never offered to help make ice cream again!

We did learn sometime later that we didn't quite have all the steps quite right. The mixture was too warm to start with. It and the bucket should have been put in the ice house for at least a couple of hours before we started cranking. It was a valuable lesson...

> *"Make sure you get ALL the instructions before you try something new."*

"I'm going to stop here for a moment because I want to read you something that I think Lydia and Bailey will really like. It was written a few ago by my sister Linda for a toastmaster's speech. I love it and it fits in very well with a lot of my stories"

The Simple Life

By Linda Pye

Recently I have read a lot about persons giving up their highly paid but stressful lives to live the "simple life."

By popular definition, this means moving out of the city into a simple home that has been paid for in full and living within a very limited income. Purchases cease except for necessities and so do commitments to life outside the family.

I can relate very easily to that lifestyle. I lived it as a child. No doubt, the "simple life" was far easier on me than it was on my grandparents with whom I lived.

They had a farm in the midst of isolation. The year I left, electricity and a phone were installed and shortly thereafter my grandma won a television set and life changed forever.

But that was later.

The "simple life" that I enjoyed so much came from the joys of freedom. Unless the weather was uncooperative, we were outdoors. We swam in the local dugouts, feasted on numerous types of berries in their seasons, rode our bikes down dirt back roads and hiked cow trails. Despite our grandmother's admonitions that we should not trespass, we loved to explore abandoned houses in hopes of finding some small treasure - a 20-year-old calendar or a broken chair. We damned the tiny streams that flowed across the driveway and created lakes, which really pleased the adults.

One favourite activity was climbing the gigantic spruce tree from which our swing hung. From there you could view the

world for miles around. Unfortunately, my grandmother quickly learned to look for me there and so I had to find other secret places. The ice house was perfect! It was constructed of logs and I could observe the yard by peering through the cracks without being seen. Of course, my grandmother always knew where I'd been by the sawdust that covered my clothing.

Spruce tree & Ice house behind us

Have any of you ever harvested ice? Back during that "simple" time when we had no electricity, it was difficult to keep food in summer. We had an icebox that required ice to be placed in the upper compartment.

Similar to this picture

We gathered our own in mid-winter when the ice was a couple of feet thick on the lake. Hugh rectangles were cut and hoisted onto the back of the pickup. It was then unloaded in the ice house and blanketed with mounds of sawdust.

Winter was filled with many activities. We skated on the

dugouts. My uncle made us a blade for clearing snow out of a half sheet of plywood and it wouldn't take long before another area had been cleared for a makeshift hockey game. Sometimes, we'd have neighbourhood skating parties after dark. People would drive their vehicles up to the banks and shine their lights onto the ice. Bonfires were lit and everyone joined in the scrub game - even if they didn't have skates.

We also cross-country skied, rode sleighs down the hills and build igloos out of the snow. We had one road passed the farm that usually had six feet high drifts which were frozen hard enough to walk on. Many a day would find us "toasty" warm in our under snow clubhouse.

When we first moved in, the upstairs of the house was unfinished - just one large room with open rafters. That was a child's dream! My heart skips a beat now when I think of how we used to crawl on rafters above the stairs, just daring ourselves to fall. I don't recall that we ever did.

A child equates love with security. Two everyday occurrences used to bring me great comfort. The first was the ritual lighting of the gas lantern. It hung over the dining room table. It was my granddad's job to light the lamp but never until my grandmother had decided it was dark enough. She used to call him "Dad," I guess it was a carryover from the time her children were little. "Dad," she would say, "I think it's time" and he would dutifully respond by reaching for the lamp and begin the process of priming it and lighting the mantles. Then he would rehang the lamp in the window to welcome anyone passing by.

Unbelievably, the second activity that brought about the feeling of security was bedtime. This was particularly true on wash day for that was also bath night. The round galvanized tub would be placed in the kitchen beside the woodstove so that we wouldn't get cold. Water would be heated on the stove and mixed with too little snow or rainwater so that we came out a bright shade of pink. We were then dressed in flannelette pajamas and tucked into sheets fresh from the line. I'd snuggle under my quilt of many colours and listen with pleasure as the wind blew the trees outside my window.

I, too, had my nightly ritual. My grandmother had a coat made from a black bear and it hung on a pedestal in the corner. After my grandmother had left and taken the coal oil lantern with her, I was always sure that that coat came to life. So, I'd turn my flashlight on a couple of times without warning to catch it sneaking across the floor. And finally, satisfied that it was, indeed, just a coat for one more night, I'd snuggle down and bid the world goodnight.

Yes, life was simple for me back then. It was simple and secure, and superb in every aspect. And that style of life beckons me still.

Beasts and the Bees

One thing you could always count on when growing up in the wilderness was lots of visitors dropping by – some you were pleased to see, some dangerous, some annoying and some of them not all anxious to share their territory with you.

I'm not talking about another homesteader stopping in on his way to get his mail every couple of weeks or so. Not the lady out riding her horse on a nice sunny day. Not even the neighbours looking to borrow a tool or get help fixing something.

No, I'm talking about the beasts of the forests.

Bears would wander by every now and then but usually, if you didn't bother them they wouldn't bother you. We had to be extra careful in the spring because coming out of hibernation the bears were very hungry and would eat almost anything and could get a little grouchy. Bears have an excellent sense of smell, so to keep them away from the yard area our garbage was placed well back in the bush.

One actually did come limping down our driveway one spring day. He was grunting and snarling and clearly was not in a good mood. The bear had either been injured or wounded and was obviously in pain. We learned early on that a wounded animal can be a dangerous animal. You can't feel sorry for it. For the safety of all of us there was  only

Uncle Paul, Linda & I

one thing to do. Uncle Paul took down his rifle from the wall and put the bear out of his misery. Actually, bear meat tastes pretty good and you can do wonderful things with the hide.

Late summer and early fall, during garden growing season, was the best time to see deer. They would just hop the fence and help themselves to their choosing of fresh vegetables. Deer are very skittish and the moment they saw you they would bound back over the fence and hide until you were out of sight.

If you looked carefully, mainly in winter or early spring, you might see a moose or two hiding in the bushes – checking out the farmyard for any hay they might get a meal out of. It was strange though, they never came around during hunting season. Maybe they sensed that moose was our favorite meat and Uncle Paul was a pretty good hunter!

Many of the smaller animals were more pests than anything else. On any given morning you could see a fox or coyote sneaking around the chicken coop trying to nab a plump chicken. Muskrats and beavers would get into the water supply and mess it up. Weasels loved eating chickens and their eggs. Don't forget rabbits – they could clean out your garden real quick but they were also tasty eating and we had many a good meal of fried or stewed rabbit.

And then there were the birds. Birds we like to see – robins, chickadees, whiskey jacks and numerous varieties that we didn't know what they were – would flit in and out of the yard on a regular basis. There were 3 that would drive us...OK, me....nuts – woodpeckers, crows, and magpies.

Woodpeckers were at their worst early morning, in the springtime. Looking for mates they would do their drumming for hours on the loudest piece of wood they could find and for some reason that always seemed to be the one closest to my bedroom window. The crows would never quit cawing!! Along with the squirrels, this group of feathers and squawks would be up at the crack of dawn seemingly needing to tell everyone in the world where they were. No sir, they and I were not friends – we waged many a battle with rocks, bow and arrows and slingshots but to no avail. They seemed to know of my reputation for accuracy and just sat there and taunting me, score = crows 1,000, me 0. All of us did not like the magpies – not only were they loud squawkers but they stole anything that had a shine to it.

Insects! There were dozens of insects, bugs, and beetles that would invade our space and either get shooed away or squashed with a mighty blow. Two that were in the most pesky and 'get out of my life' zone were mosquitoes and bees.

There was nothing you could do about mosquitoes. They would buzz; you would swat. They would bite; you would scratch. End of story. All you could do was put on calamine lotion if the itching got too bad and hope for a short mosquito season.

Bees! You want to talk about bees? I know some of them aren't actually bees but if they flew and buzzed, to me, they were bees and I was deathly afraid of them. People would say, "If you leave them alone, they will leave you alone."

Well, that was only partially true. To demonstrate that the fuzzy bumblebees were

Friendly Bumble Bee & Ornery Wasp

friendly, Paul, when he caught one in the house would let it sit on the back of his hand while he took it outside. Honeybees are also not interested in humans, only flowers. Because they can only sting once they will tend to ignore you unless they feel threatened.

However, wasps – yellow jackets, hornets, black and whites – can be just downright mean and don't need much of a reason to go after you. They can also sting multiple times and it can really hurt.

Well, I got stung lots of times leaving them alone and just minding my own business – riding my bike, playing in the grass, walking into a building or jumping into a haystack. It was bad enough getting stung on the ankle, leg, arm or back but try getting a stinger stuck in your throat, ear, nose, lip or eyebrow. After a while, I was no longer in the 'live and let live' camp – if they got too close the battle was on.

If a bee just flew by I was ok with that, but if he turned around and came by for a second look he would have my attention and I would get ready. Should he return for a third flyby and get close to my head I would attack – swatting with my hat or hand as fast as I could. Occasionally I was successful but most of the time it ended with me highballing for the house as fast as I could run – sometimes successfully and sometimes not.

We got very good at spotting bees nests. We would make sure we never went anywhere near any nest we saw. Whenever we entered any building it became a habit to look up and check the roofline for wasp nests. If one was spotted Uncle Paul would take care of it. He would wrap an oily rag around a stick and light it and hold it under the nest. The smoke would put the bees to sleep or make them unconscious. He would wait a few minutes until the buzzing had quit and then he would knock the nest to the ground. He would then pour gasoline on it and burn the nest up – my favorite part!

However, one time, they got even – big time. At the bottom of the stairs going to our bedrooms was a window. Sometimes, just to be sneaky, rather than walk all the way to the door, I would tiptoe down the stairs, quietly open the window and climb through.

This particular day the moment I hit the ground there was an immediate multiple buzzing's flying around me. It had never occurred to anyone to check this side of the house because no one ever went there. Right above the window high in the rafters was a very large wasp's nest and they weren't happy about being disturbed.

Of course, the first thing I did was to start waving my arms all over the place trying to shoo them away but that made them just madder. "Ow," the first hornet stung me on my arm. "Oww," the second one got me on the neck, then a third and a fourth. By now I was on a dead run, going just as fast as my little legs would move, heading for the porch door – with the bees still chasing and stinging me.

Thankfully Gramma had the door open for me and closed it as soon as I burst through keeping the angry critters on the outside. Linda had closed the side window before any bees had come inside so I was finally safe. I had been stung about a dozen times – all around the upper body and head areas. I swelled up so bad I think even Linda felt sorry for me!

And people wonder why I don't like short sleeve shirts and flinch when a bee flies by!!

"Often you can see big trouble coming; it's the pesky small ones you have to watch out for"

Swimming & Bloodsuckers

"Who wants to go swimming?" was always met with an enthusiastic, "We do!"

Not only was it a great way to cool down on a hot summer day, it solved a couple of other problems too. During the winter we could get away with just Saturday bath nights but not during non-snow seasons. With all the mud, dirt and dust – particularly the dust, one could get dirty real quick. And don't forget to add in the sweat from working or playing real hard – you could get to feeling real yucky by late afternoon. So a quick dip in a dugout or swimmin' hole was a welcome relief. The only problem was that Linda and I didn't know how to swim, so we were stuck just dipping and washing around the edges, but that was about to change.

During the building of the new highway, the crews had left many dugouts, so other than the ones used for drinking or watering livestock we had quite a few to choose from. But

Example of dugout in farmer's field

you had to be careful. Bulrushes and weeds would grow around the edges of the ones that weren't looked after. Lurking in these weeds could be frogs, bugs and especially little critters called 'bloodsuckers'.

Have you ever seen one? They were round, black and could

grow to about the size of an adult's finger. If you stood in the same spot too long they would attach themselves to you, mainly on your legs but could show up on your arms and back if you stayed too close to shore. Their feet were like little suction cups and they were very difficult to pull off. The reason they were called 'bloodsuckers' is because they would bite you and burrow their way into your skin and drink your blood – just a like a giant mosquito – and the longer they were there the deeper they buried and the more difficult to get rid of.

So if you were in a non-treated dugout you had a get out of the water every few minutes and get someone to check you over. If you had one on you the first thing you did was look to see if the head had broken the skin. If it hadn't then you could pinch them between your fingers and yank them off – they would stretch out like a rubber band until one of you let go.

However, if their head had already burrowed into your skin you could not just pull them off – their head would break away from their body and remain buried and then it was really difficult to dig it out. There were two for-sure ways to get rid of them.

First, you would look to see if anyone with you was smoking. If they were you would get them to touch the bloodsucker, as near to the head as they could, with the lit end of the cigarette. This would cause the bloodsucker to remove his head, shrivel up and die – then you could easily pull it off.

The second way was to sprinkle it with pepper – when the slug sneezed its head would pop out and you could quickly grab it.... actually, you didn't use pepper - you doused it with salt. Every person who went swimming always had a container of salt in their stuff. You would sprinkle salt on it and for whatever reason this also caused the 'bloodsucker' to remove its head, shrivel up and die!

The best way to avoid these scuzzy little creatures was to get through the weeds as quickly as possible and out into the clear deeper water when they tended not to go - which was a good reason to learn to swim as soon as you could.

Similar to our swimming hole

Now unless you were just going for a quick dip, to wash the dust and grime off, you would all head to the community swimmin' hole. About 3/4 of the way to the hall there was a dugout on the edge of a farmer's field. He always left enough room so people could park their vehicles without driving over his crops. Volunteers would go there each spring and 'bluestone' the water and remove last year's weed growth. This meant dragging a block of chemical stuff (which was Blue) around the edges of the dugout. This killed all the weeds and therefore no major bugs or bloodsuckers.

There was no shallow end. One metre from the edge and the water was already over a metre deep. If you couldn't swim there wasn't much play area and no diving – who doesn't want to dive – that is the best part.

So when Uncle Paul figured we were old enough to learn, he and Aunt Barbara took Linda and me to a spot not too far from home that hardly anybody used but still didn't have many weeds and taught us how to swim.

Do you know how he did this? He used binder twine and two small empty lard pails (with sealed lids, to keep the air in), Uncle Paul placed the tins on my upper back and wrapped the binder twine around my chest and tied it behind my back.

Then he towed me out about 2-3 metres from shore. With the pails helping me stay afloat Paul showed me how to move my hands and feet so I could tread water. Once I got that figured out he showed me how to dog paddle and then he grabbed hold of my swimming trunks and lifted my back end up telling me to keep kicking my feet in small strokes and to keep dog paddling – keeping my hands under the water so I didn't slash water into my face.

Assuring me that I would not sink he released his hold on my trunks. Lo and behold, not only did I not sink but I was actually moving forward.

He swam a little bit ahead of me and then waited until I caught up to him, encouraging me to get to him, "Keep paddling, you are doing good and lower your nose so it is just above the water – you will find it much easier."

By the time I caught up to him I had built up a good head of steam and was actually moving pretty good. As I went by he reached over and untied the cans. I was so busy trying not to get water up my nose I didn't even notice until I got to the other end of the dugout.

I excitedly stood up and hollered back at Linda, "Did you see that? I was swimming!" There was no answer. Aunt Barb was not quite having the same degree of success. Linda was having a little difficulty letting her face get close to the water and every time her chin touched the water she would get afraid she was going to drown and start thrashing about – she looked more like a wounded duck than a graceful swan.

But by the time Uncle Paul had followed me back to the other end of the dugout she had gotten her confidence and was doing just fine.

As Paul and I watched her for a few moments he said to me, "Remember she is a year younger than you and not as strong so you have to keep your eye on her and help her if it looks like she is in trouble. OK?"

Satisfied that I understood he continued, "While we are waiting for them to get back here, why don't I show you a couple of other things?" With that, he showed me how to float or swim on my back so I could rest if I got tired. Linda was doing pretty good by this time and wanted to make a couple of more laps before we quit so Paul also showed me how to do the sidestroke. By the time we went home we were exhausted but we were 'swimmers'.

"Paul was ahead of his time. He didn't realize it then but he had developed a farmer's version of today's water wings."

Is it Blueberry Picking Time Again?

One thing I really disliked doing was picking berries – any kind of berries, but especially blueberries. At least saskatoons and chokecherries grew on trees. Because we weren't very tall yet we could only reach the lower branches and when they were cleaned off we were done picking. Gooseberry bushes were not much taller than Linda or I so they were reasonably easy to pick.

Blueberries, however, had high bush and low bush berries and you just know which ones Linda and I were instructed to pick. So there you were, in the bush, down on your knees, fighting the bugs and the bees, purple stains everywhere. It seemed like you could pick for hours and the can would never get full. What a terrible way to ruin a perfect sunny afternoon!

Not that they weren't good eating – they were! Once in awhile Uncle Paul would go to the neighbours and trade some of the berries for some fresh cow's cream and sometimes we would get a few berries to put on our morning cereal. Most of the time Gramma would make them into pies – I liked pies! But still, it did seem like a lot of work for one small piece of pie.

But one day Uncle Paul came to the rescue – well almost. He showed up with a new invention – a small wooden box with nails sticking out the front and a handle on top. Now you could just scoop the nails through the bush and the blueberries would fall into the box. We could pick twice as much in half the time – did I tell you yet that Paul was my hero?

An irritation did develop. There was only one box and Linda used to hog that most of the time. So next year Paul came out with a new and improved model – made from oil cans. It was sleeker, lighter and, boy, could we ever pick now. I kept waiting for him to come out with a pea or bean picker but I guess he didn't want to make life too easy for us.

There was only one problem using the pickers – we tended to also pick a lot of leaves and stems as we swooped through the bushes. Now that did help fill up our buckets a whole lot quicker but you can't eat leaves and stems. That meant when we got home we had to sit at the table and sort them out – but, at least we were sitting down.

On future berry picking days we discovered that if you gently moved the picker through the bushes you didn't break off as many leaves and therefore cleaning the berries when you got home was a whole lot easier.

And we learned –

"That sometimes going slower is the fastest way to go"

Leaves Ain't No Tobacco

One day I decided it was time that I tried smoking. Everybody smoked cigarettes! Well, almost every man anyways – Except for some of the old-timers like Grampa - he smoked a pipe. Uncle Albert didn't smoke – he used 'snus' but he only seemed to use it when he was around other men who were smoking.

I had no idea what Snus was, so one day I asked him, "What is that stuff you are sticking in your mouth – is that snuff?" - I didn't know what that was either, but I had heard the term before.

"No," he replied, "but it is tobacco." He went on to explain that 'snuff' was a tobacco powder that you sniffed up your nose. 'Snus' was a moist, smokeless ground tobacco that you usually placed behind the upper lip and sort of let it dissolve in your mouth. He gave a crooked little smile and asked, "You want to try some?"

Of course, I wasn't going to say no. He took out his tin box and showed me how to take just a pinch of it with my thumb and finger. "Now, stick it between your upper lip and gums. Don't do anything – just let it sit there and let your saliva work on it."

Let me tell you – this was not what I was expecting at all – it burned my gums and tasted downright terrible. I didn't last more than a minute before I stuck my finger in my mouth and dug it out and spitting any leftovers on the ground.

He laughed. "It does take some getting used to, I'll grant you that."

Now that 'snus' was definitely off my list forever I began to wonder if regular tobacco was just as bad. When Grampa lit up his pipe, it smelled real nice as the smoke drifted across the room. I thought maybe I should try that.

So after supper, I watched carefully as Grampa took up his pipe, put a little tobacco in the bowl, tamped it down, put in a little more tobacco and tamped it down again. He put the pipe in his mouth, held the match over the bowl and sucked his breath in, drawing the flame down to the tobacco. After 3 or 4 puffs he was satisfied the tobacco was lit and he leaned back in his chair to enjoy his smoke. I did notice that if he took too long between puffs that it would go out and he would have to relight it. It seemed like a lot of work to me so I gave up on that idea.

That left cigarettes! Many of the men in the area smoked what you would call 'roll-your-owns'. You would lay out a rolling paper in the palm of your hand, sprinkle in a dash or two of loose tobacco, fold the paper around it, roll it back and forth until it formed the right shape and finally lick the glue, on one edge to form a tube. Finally, you twisted each end to stop the tobacco from falling out. It was a little work but I figured I could handle it.

There was only one problem. Uncle Paul must have had a good year because at this time he was smoking 'store-bought' smokes – which he kept in his shirt pocket and there was no way I was going to be able to sneak one of those.

The next afternoon Linda and I were playing in one of our favorite places amongst the trees. We had cleared out a small area behind the crystal palace (outhouse). There were no windows on that side of the house and the poplar trees and the outhouse gave us good cover from most of the yard. It was a good place to remain unnoticed.

It wasn't long until I was whining to her about not being able to try smoking. She looked up from the straw and twig chair she was making for her doll to sit on, "Isn't tobacco just ground up leaves?" I nodded, "I think so."

"Well we have lots of dried leaves here, why don't you just make you own?"

What a brilliant idea! I gathered up a handful of the driest leaves I could find. I ripped them into the smallest pieces I could and then smashed them with a rock until I had a nice little pile of 'tobacco'. I tried wrapping it in another leaf but that didn't work out too well – would not roll well and wouldn't stay together – I needed paper.

The outhouse – it always had paper. Of course, the only paper there was toilet paper but it would just have to do. It was pretty flimsy so I folded it three times to give it a little strength. I spread my 'tobacco' down the middle, folded the paper over, twisted one end so the tobacco would not fall out and gently lifted it to my mouth. I found out you really can't lick toilet paper but I managed to get it wet enough that it would stick together. It was kind of big and drooped towards the end – but it looked like it might hold - time to try it out. I lit the match and held it up to the end of my smoke.

Have you ever lit toilet paper before? Don't! 'POOF' it burst into flames unraveling into small balls of fire going in every direction. I jumped! Linda jumped! Skipper jumped! Fortunately, the fire went out quickly and no damage was done – but I got a little smarter that day –

Smoking is bad and can be dangerous – DON'T DO IT!

I'm on a Threshing Crew!

If you were a farmer the first thing you checked every morning was the weather – especially at harvest time. When the grain was ready most farmers, at this time, would use a binding machine. It was a 2 man operation with the binding machine pulled behind a tractor. One man drove the tractor and the other man operated the binder.

The binder would cut the grain and then tie it into sheaves (bundles) which were dropped back onto the field. The farmer would come back later and stook them - stand 5 or 6 bundles up together – to keep the grain off the ground and allowing the air to dry them out.

This was when the weather really needed to cooperate – if it rained at the wrong time the grain would be too wet (called tough) and wouldn't separate properly when it went through the threshing machine – resulting in 'dirty grain' and lowering the price. If the wind blew too hard it could knock the stooks over, spilling the grain on the ground and the farmer could lose quite a bit of his harvest – geese were happy though!

Come Sunday, it was a real struggle to get the men to go to Church: they wanted to be out in the field in case the weather changed. The women would pressure them by saying "a little prayer in church for a good harvest wouldn't hurt." And the men didn't really mind because there was always coffee and pie after church, and it gave them a chance to huddle with the other farmers to discuss in what order the farmers' fields would be harvested.

There might only be one or two threshing machines in each community so they would form threshing crews and tackle one farm at a time. Not all fields would be ready to harvest at the same time – Grain in the valley wouldn't necessarily ripen at the same time as grain on the hill; rain might hit one farm but miss the field over; oats, barley or wheat would be ready at different times.

When our turn came and the men started showing up I stuck as close to Uncle Paul as I could. I still remembered last year when I was still too small to help in the field and had to stay back at the house – which meant I was a helper on the 'food' crew. At lunchtime or tea and supper time the ladies and younger kids – that included me – would load all the food and tea into their trucks and take it to the field where picnic tables had been set up near the threshing machine. After the 'workers' had had their fill we finally got to eat. Then it was load everything back into the trucks and get ready for the next meal.

Yes, it was important work, but one year of packing food back and forth, eating leftovers and listening to ladies 'gossip' all day was enough for me – I wanted to be in the field with the 'men'.

When I could absolutely not wait any longer I finally asked, "Uncle Paul, can I come help this year?" Paul looked over at a couple of other men and gave a 'what about it' look. One man said, "Well, George couldn't come this year so I guess he could do his job." That was it! I was hired – I was now a working man.

Most of the men, maybe 10 or 12, were already at the field by the time we got there –. A tractor had been hooked up to the threshing machine and the owner had it running to make sure everything was working properly. There were 3 teams of horses and wagons standing by ready to go.

This being my first time I patiently waited for them to get it all organized and for someone to tell me what I was to do. Finally, Paul came over, "Your job is to drive the team - do you think you can do that?"

I looked over at the two large horses hitched to the wagon. I had never driven horses before, but I wasn't going back to the food crew so I confidently declared, "You bet, just show me what to do."

Paul lifted me up on the wagon and along with two other men jumped up behind me. One wagon headed for the far edge of the field, one started down the middle and we went to the other side of the field. I watched as to how Paul gave the reigns a little flick and a 'click, click' with his tongue to get the team started. Once we got to the edge of the field he gave a little side tug on the reigns and said, "Hee" to the horse – this is how you get them to turn left. 'Haw' got them to turn right. He explained that my job was to keep the wagon between the rows, not to get ahead or behind the men throwing the stooks onto the wagon and definitely not let the horses eat the stooks.

There was one last thing, "You can't stand down here in the wagon because we are going to throw the stooks in here and you will get buried – you need to climb up there," as he pointed to the top of the wagon rails. "Just wrap your feet around the center post and you will be just fine."

I must admit, the ground looked a long way down from up there but it didn't take long before I could 'git up' and 'whoa' with the best of them. The horses were a very gentle team and well trained.

The plan was to go down to the end of the field and then back up to the thresher and unload. There was a man on each side of the wagon using a pitchfork to throw the sheaves up and one man stayed in the wagon and stacked them in an orderly way.

When we got back to the threshing machine Paul showed me where to park and then men started tossing the stooks into one end of the machine. I had never seen a threshing machine actually working before so I intently watched the sheaves travel down the conveyor belt, passed the shakers –which separated the grain from the straw - the grain being augured into the granary through a hole in the roof and the straw being blown into a pile at the other end of the thresher.

I must admit that by the time we made a loop of the field my legs were a little stiff and sore from hanging onto that wooden post but the good news was – I was now on a threshing crew and when lunchtime came they let me be first in line!

The following year, now that I was a proven veteran, I was really looking forward to being on the crew again. However, to my surprise, I had a different job. The previous year there had been something that kind of puzzled me – there was a young teenager I didn't know that never seemed to be around when we were unloading but always showed up at tea or eating time – I was about to find out why!

Paul took me over to the granary and opened the door. He pointed to the hole in the middle of the roof. This is where the grain would come through. As it was falling straight down it would form a cone shape. If you did nothing it would eventually reach the hole and spill out. My job was to shovel the grain over to the sides and corners of the granary so it filled up evenly.

For most of the morning, it wasn't too hard of a job. I would stand in a corner and wait until the grain stopped coming through the hole. Then I would climb onto the grain pile, spread the grain around, go back in the corner and wait for the next wagon.

Things went well until the granary started filling up. I quickly discovered that if I waited until the grain stopped coming in the cone would get too high and that was a problem. If I stood at the bottom of the cone and just scooped the grain away more grain would just fill up the hole I had just made – that was OK but sometimes it would trigger an avalanche and a whole bunch would come down and that was not OK. Grain is just like quicksand – if you sunk down to your knees it was almost impossible to pull your legs back out. With the noise of the tractor and threshing machine, there was no way anybody was going to hear me hollering.

That meant climbing up near the top of the pile and shoveling from there. It was farther to throw the grain but much safer. The second problem was I could no longer leave through the door. As the grain got higher and higher around the edges, boards had to be put across the door opening to stop the grain from spilling out on the ground. A window-sized opening had been cut at one end of the granary up near the peak of the roof – allowed fresh air to get in. I could climb up the cross boards until I could stick my head out and breathe some fresh air. At lunchtime one of the men put up a ladder and I was able to crawl out. I was already tired and still a half-day to go.

By late afternoon I was struggling to keep up. The top of the pile was so high that if I didn't shovel in double time as the grain was coming in it got very close to blocking the hole. At tea time Paul climbed up the ladder to see how much room we had left and to determine if we were going to need a couple of grain trucks to haul some of the remaining grain to another granary. Noticing how pooped I was he climbed in and went to work leveling the pile. It would be close, he thought, but there should be enough room to fit it all in – he was right, it was close, but we made it.

I was some tired boy at the end of the day and beginning to wish I was back on the food crew. I was already hoping that next year threshing day would not fall on the weekend and I would thankfully be in school! Turned out I got even luckier than that – Paul bought a combine – threshing days, for me anyways, were now done!

"Sometimes getting a promotion is not always a good thing."

Let There Be a Better Light

It seemed like every couple of months there would be something going on at the community hall – a wedding, Halloween party, Christmas concert or just an old fashioned country dance.

Gordondale Hall in the '50's.

Electricity hadn't come through our area yet so the hall was lit by coal oil lanterns. They were either placed on shelving or hung from the walls at numerous spots throughout the hall. The hall had only a few windows so someone would go to the hall during the daytime and open the doors to get enough light to see inside. They then would take down each lantern and fill it up with the coal oil. The first people to arrive for the function would then go around and light each one of the lanterns by raising the glass and lighting the wick which was soaking in the coal oil. You could adjust the brightness of the soft yellow flame by turning the wick up or down.

Then came the big day – the community upgraded the hall to a propane heating and lighting system. All the old lanterns had been replaced by shiny new lamps attached to the wall connected to each

other by small tubing running along the wall. Each lamp still needed to be lit individually but now you just turned a switch and held the match beneath the mantle - similar to a wick but shaped more like a small light bulb (it kept the propane flow and flame together). Propane burns much hotter than coal oil and the bright blue flame produces a lot more light.

It seemed, however, that no-one took the time to really think through what would be required to light the new lamps. A row of lights had been installed down the centre of the ceiling approximately 5 metres above the floor. This now meant that someone had to get out the big stepladder, climb it, light the lamp, climb down, move the stepladder to the next lamp, climb it, light the lamp, climb down, move it, etc...all in all, a very annoying task.

Wouldn't you know it; Uncle Paul came to the rescue. He invented a light turner-on thing-ma-jig. It was two long pieces of wood joined together at the top with a short crossbar and a candle holder attached. The crossbar had a slot cut through it. How it worked was – you raised the bar up to the light, placed the slot over the propane switch, twisted the poles to  turn it on and then lit the light with the candle. Was I impressed that my uncle had invented this? You bet I was! And what did I learn from this invention?

"With a little ingenuity and common sense you can solve just about anything!"

A Close Call

The storm had passed and the sun had come out but it was still bitter cold that morning as a slight wind knifed right through our winter jackets.

Normally we would all just stay indoors as much as possible and wait for the cold snap to pass. However, this particular morning Uncle Paul had somewhere he needed to be and that meant trying to get the truck started.

As usual, when the temperature dropped into the -30's Paul would take the battery out of the truck and keep it in the house overnight. If he didn't the cold would drain the battery's juice and it would be dead by morning.

Hoping I might get to go along I had bundled up and watched Paul put the battery back in the truck and tighten the bolts. He jumped in the truck, gave the gas a couple of pumps and hit the starter – 'irrrrrr', 'irrrrr' A couple of more pumps of the gas and 'irrrrr, irrrrr' – nothing – the engine would barely turn over – not a hint of life. This only meant one thing – the oil had started to freeze and was too thick to get up into the engine. This was not unusual in cold weather and Paul knew what he had to do.

He went to the shop and came back with the blow torch, lit it and climbed under the truck. He slowly began to pass the flame back and forth under the oil pan to heat it up and turn the oil back into a liquid.

I knew this was going to take a while and I was beginning to feel the cold so I decided to go back inside and warm up. As I walked by the truck and headed to the porch I glanced down at Uncle Paul's legs sticking out from under the truck – then I saw it – a puff of smoke up near his waist.

Just as I yelled, "I see smoke!" Paul scooted out from beneath the vehicle and tossed the blow torch to the side. He leaped into a standing position and feverishly started patting up and down the sleeve of the jacket – it didn't help. The blue flames just kept bouncing from one spot to another and looked like they were spreading. At the same time he hollered at me, "Quick, go grab a blanket!" and dropped to the ground rolling about in the snow trying to put the flames out. Luckily, Gramma had seen the commotion from the kitchen window and she came flying through the door with a blanket in her hand. She threw it over Paul and both of us patted it down to smother the flames.

"Are you alright," Gramma anxiously asked? Paul sat up and checked himself over. Other than a few singed hairs on the back of his hands and a couple of small holes in his coat no damage had been done.

Paul figured that when he was moving the torch back and forth the flames had gotten too close to his other sleeve. It was an old coat that he only used when he was working on equipment and it was soiled in oil and grease. This also helped explain why the coat caught on fire so quickly. When Paul patted the flames he actually helped spread them and they just jumping from oil patch to oil patch.

With that, Paul changed to a much cleaner coat, picked up the blow torch, lit it and climbed back under the truck – although this time with two pairs of eyes watching very carefully. A good lesson indeed -

"When around flames never wear anything that can easily catch on fire."

I knew you were going to ask – "Where was the bathroom?"
Are you sure you want to know? Well OK then -

The Crystal Palace

W hen we were very young there was a pot put under each of our beds in case you had to go to the bathroom in the middle of the night. However, once we got to school age one had better not use it for number 2 unless you were very sick or it was very, very, very cold outside and there was a blizzard happening!

The 'Crystal Palace' – I think it was called that because in the winter it was always covered in frost and snow crystals – was located about 40 paces east of the house with poplar trees and bushes beside and behind it. It was made of wood and was used by both men and women. A hole was cut in the door to let fresh air and light in.

Before Linda and I came along the original palace had only one seat in it. But the seat and hole were adult height and size and I think Gramma was worried that Linda was going to fall through so they remodeled it into a two-seater. The second seat was much closer to the ground and the hole just the right size for us.

Similar-looks inviting, doesn't it?

There were no lids on the seats so it could get quite smelly in there during hot summer days. Sure, they put lime down the hole to reduce the smell but still, you learned to hold your breath as long as possible and you never stopped long enough to read the catalogue. We men were lucky, we could just step into the bushes and pee – besides, if you were caught peeing on the seat you were in big trouble.

The other thing you had to watch out for was bugs, flies, and bees. You know, anywhere there is poop there are also bees. So before you sat down you would always bang the seat and wait for a moment – listening for any buzzing or giving them time to get away. The last thing you want is to get stung on the backside while you are sitting down.

Winter was another story. The seat was always very cold, sometimes even frozen if the door had been blown or left open and snow had gotten inside. You wouldn't stick to it but it sure would wake you up real quick. There was a small board that was about head high that went around the sides of the palace, and by hanging on to it with one hand we could hold ourselves about an inch off the seat while we did our business.

Going to the 'palace' at night was an adventure by itself – especially if there was no moon. We did have a flashlight to help us find the trail but still, you had no idea what might be hiding in the dark – a deer, a coyote, a moose or maybe a bear! Even an unseen bird fluttering through the air or a squirrel jumping from branch to branch could give one a start. I always made sure to have my trusty sidekick, Skipper, nearby to protect me from the evils of the night. We learned to be very careful with the flashlight because...

"If anything fell down the hole it was gone forever!"

The 'Sista' Wants a Bike

You know it had to happen! After Linda saw how much fun I had riding my bike she decided that she wanted one too. After a couple of hints had been ignored and she could wait no longer she just came right out and asked for one, "When can I get a bike?"

There was silence at the supper table for a moment. Gramma got up and started clearing the dishes, "I do not think that is a good idea. It is not very ladylike and besides, you are still too little to be able to ride one."

But Linda was not giving up that easily. For the next few minutes, she continued to argue. Grampa and I just sat there and never said a word – there was no way we were going to get in the middle of this. Finally, noticing that Gramma was getting just a little frustrated, Uncle Paul spoke up, and probably figuring he had a couple of years before he would have to make good said, "Tell you what, you learn to ride Brian's bike and then we will see what we can do. Is that a deal?" Realizing that was just about the best she was going to get, Linda smiled and nodded her agreement.

I hadn't been riding for more than a few minutes the next afternoon when Linda showed up. "Let me try," she said as I went flying by. Of course, I ignored her but by the third time around she was standing right in the middle the driveway forcing me to stop. "You heard what Uncle Paul said, so let me try…Please…Please!" She pleaded.

It wasn't that often that I had her over a barrel so I let the begging sink in for a moment. Thinking that Gramma was probably right that she was too little yet, plus not wanting to get her mad and maybe lose another front tooth, I decided to be a nice guy and give her a go at it. "OK, let's go out to the side road and see what you can do."

Sure enough, just like it was for me the year before, her legs were not quite long enough to reach the bottom of the pedals. Thinking that was the end of it I nicely said, "That's too bad, maybe next year," and helped her off the bike.

But she wasn't about to give up just yet. "If I can't go over the bar maybe I can go under the bar. Hold the bike steady for me please."

Not sure what she had in mind and because this was the

The bike's middle bar is above Linda's waist

second time she had said 'please' I did as she requested.

She stood beside the bike and scrunched down a bit, put one foot through the opening until it reached the pedal on the other side which was sitting at the 3 o'clock position and then stretched her shoulder and arm over the bar until she grabbed the handlebars with her hands. There wasn't much room and her leg was really bent but she was determined, "I think I can do this. Hold the bike real steady – don't let go – hang on, I'm going to try and put my other foot on the pedal and I don't want to fall over."

It didn't work very well the first couple of times we tried. Because her head and most of the body were on one side of the bike the moment she raised her foot the bike wanted to tip in that direction – it was all I could do to stop it from falling over. After a few more tries we discovered that if I stood on the other side of her and tilted the bike towards me forming a 'V' with her body and the bike, it was much easier to keep her balance.

Satisfied that she could now get both feet on the pedals it was time to see if she could actually pedal. It was very awkward at first; because we were going so slowly she had difficulty doing a full turn of the pedals without her foot slipping off. Gaining confidence we picked up the pace and soon she was doing full turns of the pedals and each time we would go a little longer distance.

By the time we had done a half dozen or so passes up and down the road, I was almost running beside her. I was still hanging onto the bike but her balance was getting better and better. We kept it a secret and continued practicing for the next few days. Soon she was riding without much help.

Finally, she could keep the secret no longer. As soon as lunch was over she turned to Uncle Paul and asked, "So, when do I get my bike?"

Startled, not expecting to hear this question so soon after the previous discussion he calmly declared, "Like I said, as soon as you learn to ride I'll see what we can do."

A big smile appeared on Linda's face, "Well Uncle Paul, I can ride now," she happily declared.

His bluff having been called Paul simply said, "Show me."

We went outside and Linda got in position. Paul's eyes got a little wide open, not sure what he was seeing. "Ok, let's see what you can do – you have to ride up to the road and back to prove you can really ride."

I gave her a little push to get her started and away she went – all the way up to the road and back.

"Well I'll be darned," Uncle Paul retorted, "I have never seen anyone ride like that before. Well done! You have proven you can do it so I'll keep my word."

Even Gramma was impressed that not only had Linda

accepted the challenge but also had the determination to succeed and agreed it was OK for Linda to get a bike. So the next time Paul went to town he talked to our dad, who bought her a really nice lady's bike – it even had fenders and a small wire basket in front!

It's a strange saying but it did prove that

"There is more than one way to skin a cat"

Inside Games

During the summer when the temperature was warm and the days were long we spent a great deal of our time outside – except when it was raining of course. But the cold, dark, snowy days of winter meant a lot of time was spent indoors. Running, jumping about, fighting and yelling were not allowed so Linda and I had to find other ways to entertain ourselves.

Reading was always an option and often we would just read our library books. Sometimes Uncle Paul would haul out a volume from the Books of Knowledge. It was like an early version of an encyclopedia set but was more interesting as it included classic stories in addition to facts. Paul would go through stories with us and help explain the stuff we didn't understand.

We had a selection of board games but card games were always a favorite and between our friends and Uncle Paul we learned how to play, among others, crib, hearts, go fish, old maid and, of course, the notorious – WAR!

Two games that Grampa liked to play were checkers and chess. But he had a rule – he wouldn't teach us to play chess until we could beat him in checkers. As we were setting up the board he would reach into his prized stash of peppermints and give us each one. I think it was partially to ease our disappointment of him always winning but it was an excellent consolation prize. Linda became a pretty good checker player but she never could beat Grampa. It took me a while but the big day finally came and he agreed to teach me chess.

He would bring out his prized ivory chess set, that he got from England, light his pipe and proceed to teach me the finer points of the game. I don't remember ever beating him. He always seemed to know 4 or 5 moves ahead of me where I was going to move but eventually, I improved enough that I could give him a decent game.

The Meccano and Tinker Toy construction sets were always a lesson in creativity and ingenuity as we would build all kinds of wonderful contraptions. Pick-up sticks taught us patience and steady hands.

I'm sure 'jacks' was Linda's favorite game - you know the one where you toss a ball up in the air, pick up the jack(s) and catch the ball before it bounces more than once. She would play it with her friends at school and practice by herself at home. She was good at it – no – she was very good at it. It didn't make any difference which variation we were playing, she would always beat me and most times, beat me good. I bet you can tell this was not one of 'my' favorites – but I played it.

When there are only two of you, you learn to play with each other or you spend a lot of time alone. Besides, I would get even by making her play 'crokinole'.

Have you ever play crokinole? The board is round and made out of wood. In the center of the board is a hole which is surrounded by a series of pegs. The idea is to place around playing piece (just smaller than the hole in the board) on your shooting area and snap it with your finger in a manner that made it slide forward, hopefully

into the hole. If your opponent had a piece on the board you had to hit it or your piece was removed. The trick was to hide your piece behind a peg so your opponent couldn't hit it. At the end of the round, you would count up the point values of each person's pieces still left on the board to determine a winner. Linda's finger would always get sore and then she couldn't shoot hard enough to knock my pieces off the board. I never told her I practiced using different fingers so when one got sore I just switched to another finger – sneaky, I know, but I had to get even for the whooping she gave me at 'jacks'!

We had a magic trick we loved to pull on guests that came to visit. We would spread out 9 objects – magazines or books – in three rows of three. Linda would then leave the room and I would get the visitor to pick one. Linda would then re-enter the room and I, using a pointer, would randomly point to different magazines and ask in the same way each time, "Is it this one?" She would reply, "No," until I pointed to the correct one and then she would proudly answer, "That's it!" Naturally, the guest would be impressed and many times asked us to do it again. Linda never missed getting it right.

Being good magicians we never told anyone how it was done – no matter how much they begged – and I'm not going to tell you either!!

OK, OK…just this one time but you must promise not to tell anyone else…agreed?

When Linda came back into the room she would watch very carefully where I would place the pointer on the first magazine I touched. If I touched it in the bottom left corner, it told Linda that the guest had picked the magazine in the bottom left corner. If I touched the magazine at the top in the middle that meant the correct choice was in the middle of the top row. I would only do it once so whoever was watching would not catch on. Good trick, eh?

But every once in a while we would have to let off a little bit of steam – couldn't be quiet all the time. We would head upstairs to our rustic sleeping areas which consisted of two rooms. A smaller area on the east end was Linda's room. The remaining area was where Uncle Paul and I slept and doubled as a storage area. There were no ceilings and a window at each end of the house provided plenty of daylight. Pillow fighting was heavily frowned upon and jumping on the beds was outright not allowed.

One alternative was a good old fashioned 'Sealer Ring' battle. "What is that?" you ask. To keep berries, vegetables, and meat from going bad they would be put through a 'canning' process. This meant they were cooked on the stove and placed in glass jars. To make sure no air got into the jars rubber 'sealer' rings were placed between the lids and the jars. When they wore out, the rings would be thrown out and new ones would be used.

Linda and I would collect these rings and turn them into weapons. Because the rings were made of rubber they would stretch – but not very much. So we would 'knot' (tie) 2 of them end to end to get more stretch and therefore be able to shoot them farther. You would put one end over your thumb and pull back on the other end, like a slingshot or rubber band, and fire it towards your enemy.

We would build forts or barricades to hide behind as we did battle. Because the rings did not fly very fast and were not very accurate, we got most of our 'hits' by deflecting them off the rafters or walls. My favorite strategy was to shoot short of Linda's fort and then when she came out of hiding to retrieve the ammunition I would have a clear shot!

"If you are bored, it is because you haven't allowed your imagination to go to work!"

Going to the Movies & More

Growing up on the farm pretty much meant you had to provide your own entertainment. We got quite good at doing that but it was tough coming up with new ways to do the same old stuff. So every once in a while Paul would surprise us and ask, "Who wants to go see a show?" You never had to ask us twice; we had our boots on before he even finished the question.

As soon as we got to the theatre Gramma always made sure we went to the bathroom – she didn't want us running around during the show. There was indoor plumbing - I liked that. Paul would always get us popcorn and soda pop – another bonus. The show always started with a newsreel about interesting things that were happening somewhere in the world. Next came the best part, a cartoon – sometimes it was Bugs Bunny, Mickey Mouse or Donald Duck – it didn't matter, they were all funny.

One of the two movies that I remembered for a long time was called 'Oklahoma'. I thought it was going to be a western but it turned out to be a 'musical' western. I didn't like this movie very much – too much singing and dancing and talking. Heck, there were not even any wagon trains or 'Injuns'. What kind of a western was that? It almost made me want me to give up my career as a cowboy!

*****

The second one was called 'Old Yeller.' It was about a boy and his adventures with a big yellow dog. Most of the movie was really good but towards the end 'Old Yeller' gets bit by a wolf and gets rabies. Rabies affects an animal's brain and they go mean. When Old Yeller started snarling and tried to attack the young boy, Travis knows he has to shoot it. It scared the 'bejeebers' out of me and I had nightmares for weeks about

'Old Yeller' crashing through my bedroom window – especially on nights when you could hear the wind howling outside. At least Linda had the flashlight to protect her from the bearskin coat (they figured I was big enough not to need one), I had nothing! I'll tell you I sure kept my eye on our dog Skipper for a couple of months, especially when he snuck up behind me. I wasn't taking any chances.

*****

Finally, electricity finally made its way to our area. One of the first places to get wired was the community hall. That opened up a whole new set of activities – including a traveling movie man. On the day of his arrival, we would go to the hall early and set up as many folding chairs as the community had.

Someone would help him carry the projector into the hall and place it on a table in the aisle between the rows of chairs. After the machine was plugged into a long electrical cord the operator would turn it on to shine a light on the screen set up at the front. The table would be moved forward or backward  until the projected light covered the whole screen. At this point, he would take a reel of film, snap it in place and thread the film through the machine to an empty reel at the rear of it.

After the operator was satisfied everything was ready to go he would ask people to take their seats. Usually, a short talk was given to introduce the topic of the movie. The movies weren't the ones that played in cinemas but were documentaries or docudramas. Sometimes they were about animals in the wild or the logging industry or the building of the Alaska Highway – anything that might be interesting to country folk.

Afterward, there was always visiting time to talk about the show and enjoy some cookies or pie – both much better than popcorn.

*****

Then came the great day that I discovered that you didn't have to go to a movie theatre to see a show, you could watch cartoons, comedies and even westerns on a special contraption right in your own home.

It started out as a normal shopping trip to the big city. Every month or so we would go to the Coop in Dawson Creek to buy groceries, clothes or maybe tools or hardware – stuff you couldn't get at the country store. The best part was we always got to have lunch in the cafeteria, usually fish and chips – our favorites.

This particular day, after lunch, Gramma and Aunt Joan told us we were going to another store, Woolworths, that was just down the street. I didn't remember being in this store before so I went exploring up and down the aisles to see what might be of interest. When I got to the back corner of the store I looked back to see where everyone else was – they weren't there. I scurried along the back row, peering down each aisle looking for a familiar face. When I got to the end of the row and still hadn't seen anyone I knew, I panicked.

Out in the country where I knew where I was, I was a brave little soul, but in the city, I was afraid of getting lost. Thinking Gramma and Aunt Joan had forgotten about me and left the store I took off at a run down one of the aisles toward the front of the store. Suddenly, WHAM, I was flat on my back!

I looked up and this old lady, no taller than me, was staring at me with a look that could break a mirror. She had nailed me across the chest with her large handbag and was now poking my arm with her walking stick. Not sure what to do I just laid there as she started shaking her fist at me and giving me the 'old what for' in a language that I didn't understand.

Thankfully, Aunt Joan was nearby and came to help me out. She knew the lady and calmed her down while she helped me up and directed me towards Gramma. Joan explained to me later that the lady was German and her husband and family had been killed during the Second World War. This had made her mentally unstable and that she hated all men – regardless of their size – and that I should not go anywhere near her if I could help it.

As they hadn't finished their shopping yet Gramma suggested maybe I should go outside and wait for them. It sounded like a good idea to me, my chest was still hurting. I didn't want to be anywhere close to that lady again. Aunt Joan showed me where the trucks were parked on the next block and told me that Paul and Albert would be back there soon.

As I wandered down the street towards the truck I saw the sign for the 'MacLeod's' store. I liked that store – it was a hardware store and always had interesting stuff in the window to look at and today was no different.

"What was that?" I couldn't believe my eyes. There were 5 or 6 boxes of different sizes, with antennas, that were showing cartoons – just like at the movies. Sure, they were in black and white, but still – what kind of miracle was this?

I stood there, amazed, watching cartoon after cartoon – this was just great! Not liking birds too much I naturally rooted for Sylvester to eat Tweety Bird and for the Wily Coyote to catch the Road Runner but I was out of luck this day! I just stood there watching in amazement – it never occurred to me that if I went inside the store there might also be sound – I didn't care; I was having the time of my life!!

Just when you think everything has already been invented something new comes along"

Slingshot & the Lucky Bird

Last year, during my cowboy and Indian days, Paul had made me a bow and half a dozen arrows. They were a lot of fun but the poplar bow kept breaking and the feathers on the end of the arrows, that help them fly straight, would never stay in place. Sure when I 'whooped' and 'hollered' and waved it around I looked very menacing but I couldn't hit the ice house when I was standing right in front of it. A good Indian hunter I was not.

So this year Paul made me a slingshot. We went out into the woods and found a nice strong 'Y' shaped poplar tree branch and he whittled it down to the right size. He attached two bands of used tire tubing to the wood and joined the other two ends together with a leather pouch – to put the stones in. The best  part – there was no ammunition to make or buy – it used rocks, and on the farm, there were lots of rocks. Sure you had to look a bit for good ones but in a pinch, any rock would do.

I spent most of the summer shooting at anything I could think of – cans, pieces of wood, ducks in the dugout, squirrels and birds in the trees. I was determined to get one of them there crows – never did! The only things I couldn't shoot directly at, besides Linda and Skipper, were the chickens. I used to aim close to that miserable rooster just to let him know I was nearby by but I knew if I hurt him I was in big trouble.

But I was not yet a successful hunter and a fellow has to earn his keep, you know. So the day I spotted a grouse up in a tree beside the old pig pen I knew this was my chance. I loaded up with all the best rocks I could find and boogied over to where he was.

I started out by standing next to the pig barn and firing a half dozen missiles – none of them landed within a foot of him. He just cocked his head, gave me an eyeful and went back to staring off into the wild blue yonder, he wasn't concerned at all. That just made me all the more determined. I went and got a ladder and placed it on the wall of the barn. I climbed until I could see over the top, I

was about 2 metres away, and fired another couple of cannonballs at him – a little closer this time but still no hits.

This time he ruffled his feathers and spread out his wings a bit like he was taunting, "You need a bigger target boy?" That was it – I was going to have that bird for supper! I climbed right up on the roof and inched my way to the peak – now I was only about a foot away and there was no way I was going to miss. He didn't seem to be overly concerned and just sat there watching me. "Dumb bird," I thought, "he don't know I have got him now."

I was lying on my stomach, just part of my head peeking over the ridge of the roof and there we were eyeball to eyeball. We continued the staredown as I reached into my pocket for the biggest rock I had. I put it into the pouch and slowly lifted my slingshot into position – I could see the bird dead center between the two forks – I had him now. I pulled back on the tubing until it almost touched my nose.

"SNAP', the rubber band broke and flew back and smacked me in the face, causing me to lose my balance and slide off the roof. I swear I heard the grouse laughing at me as I disappeared over the edge.

Luckily for me, the ground was soft and except for a bruised ego, I was unhurt. I threw the rest of my rocks at him but the results were the same – nothing but air. In a final show of defiance I raised my fist in the air and growled at him, "Curses to you, you haven't beaten me yet!" Head hanging low I headed back to the house, defeated, and knowing it was canned moose meat for supper again tonight.

"Sometimes you have to admit you have lost the battle and regroup to fight another day"

Partridge in a Tree

There comes a time in every country boy's life, when it's time to learn how to shoot a gun. Maybe it was because I was not having very good luck with my slingshot that my time came on an overcast fall morning. Paul came into the house, took down the .22 rifle and said, "There is a Grouse in a tree back by the shop, let's get our supper."

I never did learn the difference between a partridge and a ruffled grouse; they were both about the size of a chicken and looked very similar. I don't think many other people knew either – they just called them whatever came to mind.

We headed out to a group of trees beside his shop. There sitting about halfway up a poplar tree was this patiently waiting bird. Now, personally, I thought that partridges, or grouse, were not very bright. If you moved real slowly you could actually walk almost right up to them before they would take off. Whether they were on the ground, in the bushes or up in a tree they seemed to have the impression that they were invisible and just stayed very still – which I was to quickly discover was a good thing.

Paul showed me how to load the shell, how the sights worked

and how to hold the gun. First shot – nothing but air. Second shot – nothing but air. "Squeeze the trigger softly so you don't jerk the gun." Third shot – ping – I hit a branch. Fourth shot – another branch. "Maybe if you leaned up against the tree it would help." Fifth shot – airball. Sixth shot – branch.

By now I had had time to get a good look at the bird – I was sure it was the same one that I had almost gotten with the slingshot a few days earlier. I think that the bird also recognized me because he didn't seem to be the slightest bit concerned for his wellbeing.

Seventh shot – leaves. Eight shot – branch. Do you recognize a pattern here? By the time we get to the 20th or so shot I have gone from standing to kneeling to lying down. The grouse is still in the tree silhouetted against the grey sky. I may not have shot the bird yet but I had killed every leaf and branch within a foot of it.

By now I think Paul was getting worried about running out of bullets. He lay down beside me, lined up the sights and said: "squeeze the trigger." Down from the tree, I'm sure, came the most expensive bird he had ever hunted.

And do you know what he said? "Good shot, now let's go clean it." No ridiculing, no anger, no frustration – just a compliment. He ignored what could have been another embarrassing failure and instead concentrated on the success of our endeavour. On top of that, he taught me a valuable lesson –

"Don't give up – Keep trying – with enough patience and practice you'd be surprised at what you can accomplish!"

Come On! I Wasn't That Bad!

A week or so before Christmas was the 'go cut down the tree time'. By the time Gramma got Linda and me dressed for a day in the woods – long johns, shirt and pants, sweater, winter jacket, scarf, and mittens, we were so bundled up we could hardly walk, let alone tromp through deep snow. Luckily for us, Paul always pre-scouted a promising bunch of evergreens that weren't too far off the highway so we wouldn't have to 'tromp' too far.

We didn't have a very big living room so our tree was never taller than a metre. As soon as I spotted one that was anywhere close to the right size I would declare, "Let's take this one!" However, Linda was a whole lot more fussy than I was. I'm sure she had to inspect every tree she could get to before Uncle Paul would finally have to help her make a decision. Although I'm sure we weren't much assistance Paul always let us help carry Linda's tree back to the truck.

We would leave it in the porch for a day or two until all the snow and frost had disappeared and it was dry enough to bring indoors. There was a spot next to the bookshelf, in front of the window, where Gramma would put a small table stand that was perfect for the tree to sit on – it had to be, it was the only place we could put it.

Gramma would bring out a box or two of Christmas ornaments – many of them handmade and Linda would make sure they were hung in just the right spots. A couple of red and green long paper thingys were then twirled around the tree and sometimes even popcorn strings. The best part was putting the tinsel on – you didn't have to be so careful – you could just throw it almost anywhere on the tree.

Except for the ones that we got from Gramma's family in England each year no presents were ever put underneath the tree until Christmas Eve after Linda and I had gone to bed because, of course, that is when Santa would come. Normally there would be one 'big' present, maybe some new clothes and a doodad or two. Christmas stockings would be filled with nuts, oranges and Christmas candy. All of which was very rare for us to have.

This year Dad had come to spend Christmas with us. We hadn't seen him since the summer so it was a nice surprise. Because Dad was too tall to sleep on the day bed it was decided that he would sleep upstairs with Uncle Paul and I would sleep downstairs. I was okay with that – I could stay up a little longer and it was always much warmer next to the heater, and I liked that.

Sometime during the night, I woke up and naturally looked toward the tree to see if Santa had come – which of course he had! There was an almost full moon that night and I could see the tree silhouetted against the window. Behind the tree there appeared to be 2 tall skinny things. Of course, you know I had to go look.

I tiptoed across the room, making sure I didn't trip on anything or stub my toe – I sure didn't want to wake anyone up. Because they were behind the tree I couldn't get a real good look but it appeared to be 2 bundles of 2 pieces of wood tied together. Stretching as far as I could just barely read the tag near the top – 'Brian'.

My heart skipped a beat! I panicked and scurried back to my bed. Everyone knows the story about Santa's nice and naughty list – if you were on the naughty list you got a lump of coal or pieces of wood for Christmas.

I lay there going over some of the not so good things I had done in the past year. Sure, I had done some dumb things, Linda and I had got into a few squabbles and I had got into trouble with Gramma every now and then, but come on, I hadn't been that bad!

I was a little slow getting up the next morning. I had tossed and turned most of the night trying to figure out what had got me on the naughty list. Plus Dad was here and he was going to find out what a bad kid I was.

Everyone seemed quite happy at breakfast but I just sat there, occasionally glancing over towards those two bundles of wood, worrying about what was going to happen next.

The time had come - time to open our presents! Linda got a new doll. I got a tractor with a front end loader. We both got new hand-knitted sweaters. Finally, Gramma said to me, "Aren't you going to see what is behind the tree?"

This was it! I couldn't delay it any longer. I stood up and shuffled my way towards the tree. As I got close Grampa rose out of his chair and said, "Let me help you." He reached behind the tree and carefully lifted out my pieces of wood and handed them to me.

I looked them over; they had pointed tips and leather ties about halfway down. Not sure what to do I looked at Uncle Paul and reluctantly asked, "What are these? What am I supposed to do with them?"

Everybody kind of laughed, which made me feel even worse. "Those are skis that your dad bought for you and Linda."

My eyes popped wide open and my mood immediately skyrocketed – skis! I couldn't recall having ever seen skis - only in pictures books. "Wow, thanks Dad! Can we go try them out?"

If you think skating is hard just wait until you trying skiing the first time; trying to get arms and legs working together so you were going forward instead of slipping and sliding in the same spot. It wasn't long until Linda and I were swooshing through the snow – well, slowly swooshing but still having a great time. They turned out to be one of our best Christmas presents ever – maybe I hadn't been such a bad boy after all!

"Don't jump to conclusions – the first impression is not always the right one"

Combines Go Faster Downhill

Now, Paul has always been a mellow, laid back type of person. He didn't get overly excited about very much. But there was one time when I think I managed to give him an adrenaline rush. I was 10 and we were combining. At that time you pulled the combine with the tractor. Paul was letting me drive the tractor and he was standing alongside me. After a couple of trips around the field, I guess he figured I was doing OK and got off the tractor. He followed along behind the combine checking the straw or whatever farmers do when they are back there.

Now the area of the field we were now on had a gentle slope at one end - as I went over the crest of the hill and started down the slope the tractor naturally started going faster. From watching Paul drive the truck I knew that if you pushed in the clutch you slowed down. So, I pushed in the clutch. What I did not know was if you pushed in the clutch while going downhill, and with a combine behind you that you would go faster. So here I was – gaining speed, the end of the field approaching and I've got to slow down or I'm not going to make the turn and will end up in the trees.

Paul had noticed I was traveling somewhat faster than he was. I heard him yell, "Step on the brake." So I did. But that didn't seem to have much effect - probably because I still had my other foot on the clutch. Paul's voice was a little louder now, "THE BRAKE, THE BRAKE." By now I was standing up, gripping the steering wheel with both hands and pushing on the pedals as hard as I could. Unfortunately, a 10-year-old's body does not weigh very much and it was not having the desired effect.

Out of the corner of my eye, I could see a cloud of dust gaining on me – it was Paul. He had kicked in his afterburners and was going flat out. By now he was almost beside me and over the roar of the engines I heard, ".....the clutch". I yelled back, "I'm pushing as hard as I can." There was no mistaking what I heard next - "NOOO... take your foot off the clutch." It didn't make much sense to me but it was his tractor and I was willing to try anything about now, so I took my foot off the clutch. Lo and behold the tractor gave a lurch and slowed down.

After Paul had climbed back onto the tractor and we had safely made the turn, Paul explained to me how the clutch worked and how to work the throttle and how to pump the brakes. One more trip around the field to make sure I understood and Paul again got off the tractor and let me do the combining on my own. What a boost in confidence that gave me. Although, I did notice he stayed a little closer for a while. And what did I learn from this?

"Learn to look ahead, expect the unexpected- learn as much as you can about what you are doing and - never push in the clutch when you are going downhill."

Gramma – 1: The Bear - 0

Linda and I were up visiting Uncle Stan and Aunt Barbara one afternoon and this time Gramma had come along. Linda and Gramma were in the house with Barb and I was out in the shop area pestering...I mean, helping Stan do some very important stuff.

We were interrupted with a sudden banging and clanging and a whole lot of whoopin' and hollerin', "Go on – get out here, shoo, shoo, go on git!"

"What the...?" Stan muttered. There were some bushes and a granary between us and the house and we couldn't see what was happening. Both of us took off a run to find out, "What the ....," was going on.

As we passed the corner of the granary Gramma came into view, her arms waving about with a piece of tin in one hand and a big stick in the other, still banging and hollering. Between her and the Crystal Palace (outhouse) about 6 or 7 meters away was a medium-sized black bear, not moving but in a definite stare down with Gramma.

Stan stopped and put his arm in front of my chest and whispered, "Don't move, he hasn't seen us yet and we don't want to startle him."

I don't know about you, but I think he was already startled. Here he was, a 2-3-year-old rough and tough bear and yet some short, grey-haired old lady was giving him a hassle – yep, I think he was already startled!

Stan glanced towards the house, another 30 or 40 metres away. Barb was standing by the porch, just out of sight of the bear, with a rifle in her hands. Stan put up his hand, motioning for her to stay put for now.

The bear, deciding he had had just about enough of this noise and was going to show Gramma who was boss, stood up on his hind legs and stretched his front paws in Gramma's direction.

This did not deter Gramma at all. She reached down, grabbed a handful of gravel and threw it at him. His bluff called, the bear gave a little snort as if to say, "Good thing for you I have already had lunch. That banging has given me a headache; I think I will go have a nap." With that, he dropped back onto all fours, gave one more glance at Gramma and slowly ambled off towards the bush.

Stan exhaled in a sense of relief but still spoke sternly to Gramma, "What were you thinking Mother? He could have charged you at any moment."

She looked Uncle Stan square in the eyes, "Maybe so, but when I gotta go… I gotta go and he was between me and the biffy."

For a moment, I think Stan sympathized with the bear. He also knew he wasn't going to win so he just shrugged his shoulders and said, "OK, go. We will watch to make sure the bear doesn't come back.

I didn't remember ever seeing Gramma wound up like that before but I sure knew that I would never, ever get between her and wherever she wanted to go. I was also beginning to understand where some of Linda's feistiness came from.

Don't always back down from a bully – sometimes a little 'huff and puff' can win the day"

Gumbo or Snow

You hear people talking about the four seasons and you naturally think of spring, summer, fall, and winter. Linda and I saw them slightly different – there was Mud, Fun Time, Getting Cold and Snow.

We loved summer – playing outside, going swimming, bike riding, and picnics. The days were long, the evenings were warm and we got to stay up late.

Fall was ok – fresh garden vegetables, days were shorter but it was still warm enough for bike riding, we could see the stars before we went to bed and it was hunting and butchering season – that meant for a while it was non-canned moose meat and unsalted ham.

Spring was another story – yes it was nice to feel a warm breeze on your face again but it was the season for slush and mud. Much of the soil in our area was a mixture of dirt and clay. Clay doesn't absorb water like regular dirt does so for maybe a month we were trying to slush our way through puddles of snowy ice water – it was rubber boot time – or as we called them 'gumboots.' That was because as it warmed up and the frost came out of the ground the water would mix with the clay

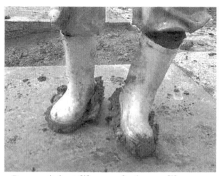

It wasn't just like mud - it was like crazy glue mud

and turn it into a real slippery and sticky 'gumbo'. If you didn't keep moving and you hit a soft spot that 'gumbo' would suck your boots down and hold you like you were stuck in cement.

Linda discovered this the hard way. She was walking very gingerly, trying to pick safe spots to step in, when her boot became stuck and wouldn't let go. Before she could stop herself she walked right out of her boot, throwing herself off balance and landing face-first into a very dirty puddle. I thought it was hilarious! Naturally, she did not! From then on whenever she got bogged down she would just stop and holler for help and somebody would have to go and rescue her – except me – she wouldn't let me anywhere near her. Does she think that I would 'accidentally' drop her in the mud? I would have never done that – honest!

We did get a job to do though. Because the water did not soak into the ground very well and we didn't have a good drainage system we would end up with small pools in the driveway and yard. Our job was to make small ditches and get the water running towards the bushes.

I don't think Linda understood the concept at the beginning. She liked to build dams. She would dig a small trench and as soon as the water started to trickle she would move a metre or so away and dam it up to make a new pool. As soon as it started to fill up she would move on to the next one. By the time I came back from working on the driveway, she had dams all over the front yard.

The other thing she liked to do in the spring, or after it rained, was play in the mud – maybe not the usual thing you would expect a young lady to do, but she had a creative side. She had discovered that you could mold wet clay into almost any shape you wanted and when it dried it would stay that way. She would build little houses, furniture, all kinds of things. And of course pretend baking – bread, cookies – I ate so many mud pies I actually developed a taste for them.

I don't think Linda minded winter, probably because she got

to stay inside most of the time. Me – it was my least favourite time of year. There was no swimming, no exploring and most important - no bike riding. Instead, you had to get all bundled up, until you could hardly move, just to waddle your way through the snow to collect the eggs and feed the chickens. Carrying wood from the woodpile to the porch every day was bad enough but when you first had to dig it out, bang the snow off and then trudge along an uneven path with an armful of cold wood – let's just say that 'nope', winter was not my favourite time of year but it came every year so we made the best of it.

Linda and I were sick a lot during the first year the school bus ran. It was the first time we had been exposed to so many other kids during the winter and we caught everything that was going around – the measles, mumps, chickenpox, flu, and colds. We drank lots of cod liver oil, (YUCK!!) were being smothered with Vick's vapour rub and received a number of visits from the traveling nurse that year – more dog-gone needles than I ever wanted.

There were some upsides to being sick and staying home though – we didn't have to ride the cold, cold school bus, we didn't have to do any outside chores and the traveling library van would stop by every now and then to give us new books to read. The best part was when Aunt Barbara would bring over homemade gingerbread houses to make us feel better.

Whenever the weather was nice, and we weren't sick, Gramma would 'shoo' us outside to get some fresh air. One of our favorite activities was building snow forts – well not so much building – although Paul had shown me how to cut snow blocks and build an igloo – we spent more time tunneling into snowdrifts.

Because there was an open field next to the side road the blowing snow would sometimes create drifts on the road that were taller than the average man and so hard you could walk on them without falling through. We would start on the side

protected from the wind and start
digging tunnels and hollowing out
sitting areas. I say 'areas' because
'ladies' are never happy with just a
one-room house – or fort! We
would cut in small windows to let
the light in. And yes, sometimes we
did have to cut blocks to shore up
the doorway or some walls.

Teresa & Leona digging their cave

It was an ongoing project
because either another storm would come in and cover it over
or the warmth of the sun would melt some of it and we would
have to start over.

After a big snowfall, Paul would use the tractor to plow out
the yard and driveway. Grampa would follow behind to shovel

the loose snow around the
edges. Sometimes, the
snowbanks were over his
head in height. Then Paul
would hook the tractor on
to a 'stone boat' (used for
hauling stones in the field)
and drag it across the yard
and driveway to smooth
out the ruts and pack the
snow down. Paul would let Linda and I ride on the stone boat
because it was fun and to give it a little extra weight.

You know, sometimes a fella should not be quite as curious as
he thinks he should be – and on this particular day, I was going
to find that out.

Linda and I were sitting on our knees, up near the front of
the stone boat. We were making our second trip up the
driveway when I noticed that the snow would build up slightly,
between the runners, and then disappear underneath us. I

began to wonder – "What if I stuck my legs out in front of the stone boat? Could I build up enough snow that it would spray over the ledge and give Linda a snow bath? I had to try, right?

I stretched out my legs and dug the heels of my feet into the snow. It worked really well for about a split second. Then the pressure got too great and the snow dragged my feet under the stone boat. I hung on for a few moments desperately trying to free my legs but it was a losing battle and I could feel myself being pulled forward – would I live if I was pulled under and the stone boat was dragged over me?

It was a question I did not want the answer to so I started yelling at Uncle Paul to stop. Linda noticed my predicament and also started yelling. Paul looked back to see what the commotion was all about and quickly stopped the tractor. By this time there was not much of my butt that was still on the boards. Paul couldn't pull my legs out so I had to flop forward onto my face so he could lift the stone boat off of me and I could roll out of the way.

Embarrassed but not hurt, and receiving instructions of not to do that again, I climbed back on and we continued our joy ride. I couldn't help noticing that Linda was having a quiet laugh to herself – I'm sure she was remembering back to when she was stuck in the mud and was very much enjoying the payback!

I now understood what "Curiosity killed the cat" meant

Old Time Hockey

Similar - add in more snow

Saturday afternoon, or sometimes Sunday after church, depending on the weather were skating and hockey times.

The community rink was outdoors and it had no boards so I don't know if you could actually call it a rink – it was a dugout just across the road from the hall. Whoever got there first would take the shovels and homemade scrapers and clean off the snow and toss it to the sides all around the rink.

The younger kids, whether you had skates or not, would get their turn first to skate, play tag, keep-a-way or whatever they chose – except play hockey. You could, however, if you had a hockey stick, skate around and pass the puck back and forth but you had to be very aware of the smaller kids and not run into them. I was very lucky that I indeed did have a hockey stick – a couple of years back at the community Christmas party I had traded my gift from Santa, of a hairbrush and comb set for the hockey stick.

Once the sun started to set, the men with older kids or no

kids would start showing up. Because there was no electricity and therefore no light they would park their vehicles all around the rink – they would drive up on the snowbanks just far enough to shine headlights slightly upwards and not into people's eyes. The younger kids and spectators would then spread themselves around the rink – if a puck landed in the snowbank it was their job to dig it out and toss it back onto the ice.

Once enough men had shown up to form even teams they would split into 2 groups and the game would begin. Other than skates and a stick no one had any protective equipment at all and you didn't want anyone to get hurt so the rules were simple: no slap shooting or raising the puck (you didn't want to break anyone's headlights or windshield), nobody checking, and last, play fair – there were no referees and no penalty box. A spectator volunteer would come out and drop the puck for face-offs.

This was my 3rd or 4th year doing this and I had just turned 11 so I had this all figured out. I would hang out around the center area – not many pucks landed in the snow there and quite often I would get to drop the puck at center ice. It was a great plan until the day they were one player short.

As they stood around debating whether they should wait a little longer, or whether one of them would sit out and they would spell each other off, one man noticed me standing nearby. "What about letting Brian play goal, he's almost big enough and he won't get hurt there?"

They all quickly agreed that that would work. The next thing I knew they were strapping a Christmas catalogue around my shins to protect my shins from wayward hockey sticks and bouncing pucks.

I proudly took my place in goal and the game began. There weren't a lot of pretty plays, it was farmer hockey, lots of jostling, digging pucks out of the snow and of course lots of goals – I didn't care, I was having a great time.

Then…for some reason all the players were on one side of the ice, up about where the blue line would normally be, scrambling to get control of the puck. It squirted loose and flew across the ice right onto the stick of big Ern who had gone unnoticed on the other side. He had come from his goal area and was just motoring.

Now Ernie was a real nice guy but he did have a reputation – he had difficulty stopping and was even worse at turning corners, maybe that is why he normally was a slow skater and didn't rush up and down the ice too much.

When I say Ernie was big, I mean big – he was about an axe handle wide and so tall he blocked out the light of the moon. All I could see was this huge black shadow hurtling towards me like a runaway train.

I said a quick prayer and got prepared to meet my maker when out of the corner of my eye who should appear – Uncle Paul. He flew across the ice just in time to give 'Big Ern' a gently nudge, sending him harmlessly into the snowbank. It was then and there I decided not to become a professional goalie.

"Sometimes, knowing what you 'don't' want to be is very helpful in deciding what you 'do' want to be when you grow up"

Chickens Don't Like Firecrackers!

It was the middle of October. It was also the second year of being bussed to Spirit River to school. By now I had made some good friends and would hang out with them during recess or at lunchtime playing soccer or just messing about. One day, at lunch, one of them approached me and said, "Come on, I want to show you something."

We ran over to the corner of the schoolyard towards the skating rink, on the side of the school that had no windows and where there was nobody around at this time of day. Bill reached into his pocket and brought out this little round oblong thing.

"What is that? I asked.

Haven't you seen a firecracker before?" I shook my head, "No, what does it do?"

He reached into another pocket and pulled out a match, "Here let me show you – first you light the fuse and then you throw it." I watched as it flew through the air and 'bang' it exploded – not a big bang but still, I thought that was pretty cool.

"Here, you try it," he said as he handed one to me. I lit the fuse and gave it a mighty throw – 'bang'. I laughed, "That was fun!"

"You think that was fun wait until you see this." He looked all around to make sure no one had heard or seen us and reached back in his pocket. This time he brought out one about 3 times the size of the first ones. "Those were called 'Ladyfingers' but this one is called a 'Blockbuster' – watch this!"

This time he threw it even higher, 'BANG' and it burst into a dozen pieces. "WOW," I exclaimed, "Where did you get those? I have to get me some!"

"At that little knick-knack store down the street"

"But how - We are not supposed to leave the schoolyard."

Bill explained that if you snuck around to the backside of school you could get across the street and around the corner without anyone seeing you.

A master plan was starting to form. I knew I had to tell Linda what I was going to do because if she saw me sneaking off there would be too many questions. So, on the bus ride home I filled her in. To my surprise she was all for it, on one condition – she got to come along. If I was going to buy something, she wanted to buy something too. The problem was we had no money! We knew we couldn't ask for it. Even though we didn't fully understand the value of money we knew that we did not have a lot of it and there was no way they would give it to us for something so foolish.

There was only one thing to do – shhh, don't tell anyone, but there was a small glass bowl on the bookcase that Uncle Paul would throw his change in. Surely he wouldn't miss 30 cents. It took a couple of days but finally, there was no one around and I could get a look inside the bowl – there were a couple of quarters and lots of pennies, nickels, and dimes, so odds were he might not notice if some of them went missing.

Naturally, being 'smarter than the average bear' I convinced my sister that she was quicker than me and she should do the scooping. Wanting to prove me right she picked her moment, strolled by the dish and with lightning speed grabbed some coins. She WAS faster than me – must have been all that practicing at 'jacks'.

The next day, at lunch, Linda and I met at a prearranged spot along the backside of the school. We waited a few moments to make sure no teachers were watching and then we scurried across the street and down a back alley. She didn't have any interest in firecrackers but had her eye on something in the store next door.

Not used to being in a store on my own I inched my way to the counter and shyly asked, "How much are the blockbuster firecrackers?" I had enough from my share of the loot to buy 2 with a couple of pennies left over, which I promptly spent on candy – I mean, what else was I going to do with them?

I could hardly wait until Saturday, dreaming of how I was going to blow up the world. Finally, it was here – It was quite chilly that morning so Gramma made me bundle up and put on the knitted mitts she had just made for me. I got my chores done real quick and then headed down the side road – far enough away that I figured no one would hear the noise.

I took out one of my ill-gotten gains and held it admiringly in my hand. I took the glove off of my other hand so I could light the match. I gave it a flick with my thumbnail and watched it burst into flames. I touched it to the fuse and watched it sparkle until it was about halfway burned. Then I reached back and gave it a mighty throw.

"BANG" As I watched it fell back to earth. I must admit I was a little disappointed – sure it was somewhat exciting but still – it just wasn't the same without anybody around to share it with. What was I going to do with my second, and last, one? I didn't want to waste it. Maybe I could find something to scare.

Nope, Skipper had abandoned me, there was not a crow in sight, in fact, no birds, not even a chick-a-dee – what was I going to do? Then a brilliant idea flashed through my brain. Of course

– it was perfect – time to get even with that rooster who had been terrorizing me all summer.

I snuck around to the side of the chicken coop and had a quick look around. Most of the chickens were outside but not the rooster. He was probably inside the hen house encouraging the remaining chickens to get outside. I wasn't worried about scaring any of the chickens. Now that it was close to winter, much cooler and a lot less sunlight they weren't laying many eggs. There were a lot of days they didn't lay any eggs at all so if another day or two went by with no eggs no one would even notice – or so I thought.

I opened the door a bit and peeked inside. Sure enough, the rooster was on the floor in the far corner. As soon as he saw me he turned, cocked his head and gave me his evil stare.

Similar- ours was a little bigger

Perfect, I thought, I've got you now!

I closed the door so he would think he was safe and stay where he was. Quickly checking again that no one was watching I loaded my remaining thunderbolt into one hand, took off my glove and struck the match. I opened the door a crack and stuck my hand through.

At precisely that moment Gramma appeared at the front door of the house and hollered, "What are you doing there?" 'BANG' - not having left my hand yet the firecracker went off – blowing a hole in my new mitt and singeing the palm of my hand. "Oww," I yelled as I yanked my hand back and tossed my still smouldering mitt to the ground.

I will spare you the details but needless to say, Gramma quickly figured out that Linda (she had already been caught with her lamp) and I had been in cahoots in scooping the money. We were in big trouble and going to be doing extra chores.

The worst part was that I never even got to see the shock on that rooster's face – but I did notice that he gave me a wide berth for a long time, so it was well worth it!

"We are not always as smart as we think we are"

Hay Bales have No Balance

It was getting late in summer when one Saturday Paul caught me out riding, "I am going to the upper field to get some hay bales, why don't you come along and give me a hand?"

Well I never turned down the chance to go anywhere with Uncle Paul so I quickly parked my bike and hopped in the pickup truck. The field was only a little over a kilometre away so it didn't take very long to get there. When the field came into view I looked out through the side window, "Wow, that's a lot of bales," I said looking at Paul.

He grinned, "Oh, I'm going to sell most of them. We're just going to take whatever I can fit into the back of the truck."

He stopped by the first bale and got out. With one hand still on the open door, he looked back at me and motioned with the other hand, "Slide over – you can drive."

"Yes sir," I excitedly replied and promptly slid in behind the steering wheel. I guess that seeing I was eleven now and tall enough to both look out the windshield and operate the brakes Paul had decided I could drive the truck.

"You remember how you drove the combine last year?"

I nodded. "Good, well the clutch and brake work the same way so just drive slow. Wait until I have loaded this bale into the back and then drive up to the next and stop until I get it loaded, OK?" Again I nodded. I knew I had this – I didn't tell Paul but earlier that summer Aunt Barbara had given me some driving lessons when we were going to pick berries –it was the only good thing about going pickin' berries!

I listened for the 'thump' of the bale in the truck box, watched in the mirrors as Paul shifted the bale into position and waited for him get up beside the truck before I started driving slowly down the field. Everything went smoothly. He filled the truck box first and then added a second layer turned sideways. The third layer he turned in the same

Paul's truck was an older model than this

direction as the first layer – this helped them cling together. The fourth layer he only made it two wide and the top layer was just a single row of bales so the load was peaked – just like the roof on a house – and made the load more stable and less likely to tip over.

Paul jumped onto the running board on the passenger side of the truck and instructed me to drive back to the main road – he wanted to make sure the load was stable and nothing was going to fall off. I drove up to the approach of the main road, stopped and went to slide back over to the passenger side. Paul put his hand out, signaling me to wait, stepped off the running board and opened the door. Then he smiled and said, "You have done a good job. Why don't you drive us home?"

I sure wasn't going to argue! After checking to make sure no traffic was coming I slowly pulled out onto the road. Paul mentioned that because the road fell off towards the ditches I should stay closer to the centerline, so the load wouldn't shift, and that he would watch out for any traffic coming up behind us.

I kept the truck in first gear, but just as the combine did, as I went over the crest of the hill the truck began to pick up speed. Paul reminded me to pump the brake and slow down to make the turn onto the driveway. I misjudged my speed and went a little too far before I started my turn. Afraid that I was going to put us in the ditch I cranked the wheel too quickly. The truck lurched sideways and out of the corner of my eye, I saw a hay bale fly off into the ditch.

Paul got out of the truck to have a look and when he came back he simply said, "We lost 3 bales – let's go unload these ones and then we will come back out and YOU can load them back onto the truck – which we did and I did! He then told me words of wisdom that I ended up using many times in my life –

"If you think you are going to miss a corner, it is much better to go by, stop and backup than it is to try to make the turn and have a mess to clean up."

BB Pistol and a Match

Who doesn't like picnics? Especially the July 1st picnic – there were races, ball games, horseshoes, bingo and, of course, you were free to just play all day. Most important was the food. All kinds of stuff we didn't normally get – like potato salad, hamburgers, hot dogs and different kinds of baked goods – and candy. Linda and I always got a dime to spend any way we wanted. Of course, that meant it all went on candy!

There was a lot of work to do to set up a community picnic – horseshoe pits needed to be raked, the ball diamond had to be smoothed out, tables and chairs arranged and ice and water put in buckets or tubs. A small group of the locals always showed up early to get everything ready and this year Uncle Paul had brought me along.

After about an hour or so 4 or 5 of the men, including Paul, had gathered at the north end of the school and were discussing what else needed to be done. As there were no other kids to hang out with I wandered over to join them. I got there just as one of them said, "We don't have much for the older boys to do, anybody have any ideas?"

They hummed and hawed for a few moments when one of the men suggested, "How about a shooting contest?" The immediate response was no – there would be too many people around and it would be dangerous.

The man continued, "I didn't mean with a rifle – I just bought a new BB pistol to chase squirrels away with and it's not dangerous at all. I have it in the truck, let me show you."

When the man came back he stood about 4 or 5 metres from the schoolhouse wall and fired at it. The BB bounced harmlessly off the wall and dropped to the ground. "See, it doesn't have much power at all – it will be safe to use."

"Well let's try it out then," another man said, "What are we going to shoot at?"

The first man answered, "Well, it did come with a small paper target. I will go get it – you find something to hang it on."

A quick look around didn't show anything promising. "You know," an older man said, taking off his hat and scratching his head, "I have a hay bale in the back of my truck that I think might just work," and left to go get it.

He stood it up on one end, "Might be a little low, but I think it just might do. How are we going to attach the target to it?"

Paul took out a wooden match from his pocket and stuck it through the top of the target and then stuck it into the hay bale. After some fiddling around he finally got it to stay in place. He then stepped off 4 man-sized paces and asked, "Do you think this is about the right distance?" Everybody nodded their approval.

The man with the gun, who was taller than everybody, said, "I think the target is a little low for me," and handed it to Uncle Paul as he was the shortest member of the group.

Paul looked at me and then glanced around the group, "How about we let Brian have a try? He is close to the size of most of the boys who will be shooting." After getting a round of approval he handed the pistol back to the owner, "Why don't you show him how to use it?"

The man took the pistol, loaded it and squatted down beside me, "Ever fire a pistol before?" I shook my head. "OK," he said, "here is what you do." With that he explained how to hold my arm straight out in front of me, close one eye, line the sights up with the target and then gently squeeze the trigger.

He stayed down beside me and guided me each step of the way. When I could see the center of the target in the sights I squeezed the trigger - 'POP', it wasn't much of a 'Bang', just a loud pop.

Everyone looked at the target and then back at me. I had done it – I had missed the whole target – no hole, no dent in the paper, nothing. Sensing my embarrassment the man patted my arm, "Don't worry son that was just your first try. I think your hand wavered a little bit when you pulled the trigger – the gun might be just a little heavy for one hand, try with 2 hands this time – and maybe we should move just a little closer - that is a pretty small target from here.

I could feel everyone's eyes on me as we got into the new position and he went through the instructions once more – this time showing me how to hold it with 2 hands.

"What's that?" One man asked. "What's what," a second man asked looking directly at the first man. "That!" the first man answered, pointing at the target. "I don't see anything," retorted the second man. A third man chimed in, "Is that smoke?"

And then everyone started talking at once, "I don't see anything! Where? Look to the top left of the target. I still don't see anything! Are you sure?"

Then, 'POOF', a flame appeared and started to burn the target. Everyone stood in stunned silence for a moment watching the flames get bigger until Uncle Paul chuckled, "My boy, I think you started a fire," and then they all started to laugh.

One man took off running, hollering back, "I'll get some water!" Paul hurried to the hay bale and grabbed what was left of the target and waved it about trying to put it out while he knocked over the bale to move it farther from the wall. The man returned with a bucket of water and doused the hay putting the fire out.

Turns out that although I had missed the target, I had, in a one in a million chance, hit the match right on the head, lighting it and sending the white sulfur part back into the hay bale. It had fallen down behind the target and lit the hay on fire.

After some good-natured kibitzing back and forth Paul inquired, "Should we try it again?"

"Can't," the tall man replied, "I only had one target!" The contest was over!

"Never use a match as a stick pin – especially on anything that might burn"

What's a Stepmother?

Although we visited our mother's sister and her family a couple of times we never saw our mother during our stay at the homestead. She would write Aunt Barbara on occasion, who would pass the information on to Linda, but as we really didn't know much about her it had no impact on our lives

We also got used to seeing our dad only a few times a year. We would see him every once in a while when we went to Dawson for shopping or at Christmas and some get-togethers. Though we loved seeing dad, it was our nearby aunts, uncles, and cousins that we counted on to be there for Sunday dinners and family picnics.

Then one Easter Sunday (we were 10 and 11) Dad showed up with a red-haired lady. It was unusual for a couple of reasons – you hardly ever saw someone with red hair in our area and neither Linda nor I could remember dad bringing a lady to a family function.

Dad told us he had met Margaret at a café close to where he lived. He also mentioned that she was a pretty good cook and also made phenomenal butter tarts – which got my attention right away – I liked butter tarts!

During the afternoon and early evening Margaret spent most of the visiting time talking to the adult family members but made sure to take time to chat with Linda and I. By the time they left we all agreed that she was a nice enough lady and we were happy that dad had a girlfriend.

Life returned to normal and we never gave Margaret much thought until Barbara showed up a couple of weeks later and announced that Linda and I were getting a new step-mother. "What's a stepmother?" we asked. Barbara answered, "When a Dad gets divorced or widowed and then marries again, that lady becomes a stepmom – like a second mother."

Not expecting it would change our lives a whole lot we were OK with that and never gave it a whole lot of thought. We did, however, get strange looks from our classmates when we told them we were going to miss a day of school to attend our dad's wedding – no one had separated parents in that generation.

That's Linda on the right side of the picture

The wedding was held on the Saturday of the May long weekend. Because Dad was a veteran of the Second World War the Royal Canadian Legionnaires performed an honour guard for them as they left the church. I had never seen a uniformed honour guard before and was quite impressed. The men formed two lines with their staff raised for Dad and Margaret to pass through.

We enjoyed the reception following the wedding and met some of our new (step) relatives. Afterwards, we piled into Uncle

Paul's truck and headed back to the farm.

It had been a cool and blustery day and Gramma wanted to get home before any bad weather set in.

We made it home just as a few snowflakes started to fall but Dad and our new stepmother weren't so lucky. By the time they left the dance and headed toward Grande Prairie for their honeymoon it was snowing so bad they only made it to Pouce Coupe – a small village 10 kms outside of Dawson Creek. Not the greatest of honeymoons but a good story to tell for years.

About two months later Linda and I got to spend an overnight at their place. Everything was going just fine until Dad decided he was going to cook breakfast the next morning. This greatly surprised us as we had never seen Dad cook before! The only other man who had cooked for us was Grandpa, on the rarest of occasions, and it never turned out well. We watched intently, from our perch at the kitchen table, as he took out one very large frying pan and proceeded to cook eggs, potatoes, and pancakes in it – at the same time.

When he placed our plates in front of us I saw Linda's eyes grow big and round. She stared at the plate for a moment; the eggs had broken and mixed in with the potatoes and pancakes. She glanced over at Dad as he started the next batch and then leaned over and whispered to me, "Which one do I pour the syrup on? I can't tell the difference between the three!" It didn't matter to me, I liked syrup on anything but I could sure tell by the look on Linda's face that she was hoping that Margaret was even a better cook than Dad said she was and that this was a one-time experience.

Later that afternoon Linda was very happy when Dad took us over to the restaurant where Margaret was working. I think she was hoping to get a treat to replace her memory of our interesting breakfast.

It was a cozy small dining room and I remember we felt comfortable there and full of hope that we had a Stepmother who just might bring some good leftovers home.

Sure enough, there on the counter were the biggest, fullest butter tarts you had ever seen and our eyes became round and big as saucers!! Some people like them plain. Some people like them with nuts. I like them with raisins and these ones were loaded with raisins! Breakfast was soon forgotten as we munched on our delicious treats!

"A good looking meal doesn't always taste good – but it sure does help you try the first bite!"

Lemon Meringue Pie

Dad liked lemon meringue pie. Uncle Paul liked lemon meringue pie. I liked lemon meringue pie. But that was one pie we never got at home. Sure, we had apple pie, rhubarb pie and berry pies. At Halloween we had pumpkin pie – didn't like that one at all. Christmas time always included Mincemeat pies or tarts – those were my favourites. But whether Gramma did not know how to make it, or it was not within the budget, we never got lemon meringue. There was only one place it was guaranteed that you could get that glorious treat – at the July 1st picnic.

It wasn't free – you had to buy it – each slice would cost you $.15. Normally either Gramma or Uncle Paul would give Linda and me each $.10 to buy candy with. Now you could buy a handful of penny candy or 2 chocolate bars but it was not quite enough to buy a slice of pie!

Fortunately, there was a way you could earn some extra cash. Because the ballplayers didn't want to stop the game to get foul balls they would pay you $.05 to get it for them. Retrieving 3 balls got you 15 cents, the price of a piece of pie – sounded good to me.

I hadn't spent any of my money yet so I only needed one foul ball. I stood by the fence out near first base and waited. Minutes later my mission was accomplished and I headed for the food booth. Oh, what a glorious piece of pie that was!

My craving temporarily satisfied I wandered over to where the races were about to begin. I don't know how Linda did but I was still one of the smaller boys there and even though I tried really hard in the three-leg race, the sack race and a couple of others I didn't win much more than maybe a sucker or a couple of jawbreakers. Still, I had fun but now was looking for something else to do.

I dropped by the horseshoe pits but I didn't know anybody who was playing and was just about to head towards the schoolhouse when I heard the unmistakable thwack of a baseball.

I looked up and there was a long foul ball coming right at me. Well what could I do but pick it and go and get my nickel. As soon as that coin hit my hand my stomach gave a little rumble - "You know I could really go for another piece of pie!" Who can argue with that? Sure enough, by the end of the game, I had enough for a second piece of lemon meringue.

As I stood at the counter waiting my turn I scanned the pie section to make sure there was some left – yep, there were still 2 pieces. Satisfied I was still in luck I glanced over the rest of the pies and what did I see – back in the corner of the table was a whole lemon meringue pie and a price tag sticking out of it that said $.50. I couldn't believe my eyes!

Thankfully Gramma had taught me my times-table real well and I quickly figured out that it cost me $.45 for 3 pieces but I could get 6 pieces for only a nickel more. So as I forked over my money for my one slice I asked the lady, "How come pie costs $.15 a piece but you can buy the whole pie for $.50?

She smile and told me, "We don't want to take any of the pies home so towards the end of the day we sell them real cheap so somebody else will take them home." Good to know I thought.

*****

So here we are in year 3 and I have a plan – it was a lot of foul balls to get and maybe the pies would be sold out but it was worth the gamble – I was going for the whole pie.

I knew if I didn't spend my start-out Dime on candy I would only need $.40 more cents. That was 8 foul balls which worked out to 2 a game – tough but doable.

I had also learned the previous year not to stand too close to the backstop and not stand on one side of the field or the other. The ideal place was behind the stands that were directly behind the backstop. The trick was not to watch the game but watch the batter. That way if he hit a foul ball I would be the first one to see it and know where it was going to land. I could be on a dead run before anybody else even moved. I was ready. Let's get this game underway! Play Ball!

I got my quota the first game, 2 down, 6 to go. The second game did not start out well. I only collected 1 ball before I heard the call for the races to begin. I quickly decided to skip the races this year – I needed to concentrate on the ball game; I wanted that pie. It was a good decision. With no other kids around I tracked down 2 more balls – I was up to $.35 and still had two games to go. I was starting to feel pretty good about this. Game 3 was a washout. One long fly ball that the right fielder went and picked up and one that landed in somebody's lap and they just tossed it back into the field. The pressure was on.

Game four started out well – got one in the first inning and another in the third. But then nothing, no foul balls at all. Heading into the 7th and last inning I was still one short. – it was getting late and maybe there wouldn't be a whole lemon meringue pie left and worse yet – what if there was and I was still a nickel short - the horrors - I started to sweat. And then the sweetest thing I had seen all day - a high pop fly, curving over the third baseman's head and heading towards the road. I was gone – little legs churning like a chicken trying to escape a coyote.

The ball landed on the road and rolled in between two trucks. I wasn't more than 3-4 metres away when one of the truck doors opened and a man got out, reached down and picked up the ball. As his arm went back into the throwing position my heart sank.

Excuse me Sir, I need that ball," I blurted out.

He stopped and looked at me, "Why?" he asked.

"Well sir," I explained, "I get a nickel for every ball I bring back and I'm still short one ball to get some pie. The game is just about over and this might be my last chance."

He grinned and tossed me the ball, "That's a good reason kid, here's the ball, go get your pie." After a grateful smile and a heartfelt "Thank you" I hurried back to the dugout.

Clutching my hard-earned pay in my hand I stepped up to the counter to claim my reward, "I would like some lemon meringue pie, please." She reached back to grab the pie plate with one piece still on it. "No, not that one, the whole pie – it is only $.50 isn't it?"

Lemon Meringue Pie

"Why yes it is," she replied, "Do you want me to put it in a bag for you?" Good idea I thought. That way no one will notice what I'm carrying. "That would be nice, Thank you, and would you also throw in 3 or 4 of the plastic forks." I didn't want to give her any idea that I was going to eat it myself. I took the bag and snuck around behind the wood and workshop at the edge of the grounds next to the trees. I sat down on the ground and placed the pie on my lap.

For a moment I just sat there staring at that beautiful round yellow, topped with fluffy white stuff, piece of goodness. I had been dreaming about this for a whole year and I was going to enjoy every mouthful of this.

Yeah, yeah, I know – I was being selfish. I should have at least shared it with Linda. But right now I'm thinking – why should I share? I earned it. Nobody helped me – just because they didn't know what I was up to was no excuse. No sir, I was going to eat it all by myself.

The first quarter of the pie was really, really good. The second quarter was still good but not quite as good – I hadn't thought of bringing any water to wash it down with and it was starting to stick to the inside of my mouth. I was almost through what normally would have been my fourth piece of pie when I knew I was done. My mouth was so dry I couldn't even lick my lips anymore and to top it off my stomach was so full it was starting to hurt.

I looked down at the still full two pieces – what was I going to do with them. It was too late to ask anyone if they wanted to share. They would have wanted to know how I got a whole pie and where did the other four pieces go? I would either get made fun of or finger wagged at and neither option was appealing to me. There was only one thing to do. It broke my heart but the last two pieces went un-eaten and into the trash can.

Thanks to a lousy sleep that night and a stomach ache for three days, it would be years before I could eat lemon meringue pie again. I had learned my lesson –

> *"Sometimes too much of a good thing can spoil a good thing!"*

The Last Day

Do you remember at the beginning of my stories that I mentioned that one day could change your whole life? Well, this beautiful sunny Sunday in late August of 1960 was one of those days.

It started out normal enough – get up, wash my face, brush my teeth, comb my hair and have breakfast. Even though it was Sunday there were still chores to do. The chickens didn't care what day it was, they still wanted to be fed and the eggs still had to be gathered.

I hadn't been outside very long until the words I dreaded broke the stillness of this beautiful morning, "Come on Brian, time to get ready for church."

Now, I didn't really mind church – most of the time – but it meant rewashing one's face and hands, changing in my best 'go-to-meeting' clothes and being on one's best behaviour for a couple of hours. It seemed like a terrible waste of time for something that didn't really interest me at the time. Plus, you really never knew what the service was going to be like.

Being a small farming community we didn't have our own minister. They would come from different churches, in Dawson Creek, on a rotating basis and hold services in 3-4 communities on the same day. Many of them were younger and just learning so sometimes it could get quite interesting.

However, there was one, a real nice man, but one I was never quite thrilled to see. His sermons never ended in an hour. A quick one was an hour and 15 minutes – a normal one lasted almost an hour and a half. And did he like to pray – you could have a short nap during some of his many prayers.

I was pleased that to find out this was not his Sunday and even more pleased to find out that Aunt Barb was going to teach Sunday school this day. Eight to ten of us gathered in an out of the way area and got to listen to Aunt Barb tell us Bible stories for the next hour – all in all, a decent day so far.

Until, just as the service ended and Aunt Barb had finished her last story, she glanced around the class and said, "Say goodbye to Brian and Linda as they are moving to Dawson Creek today."

What? What? My eyes glazed over and my mind was churning at a hundred miles an hour as I tried to digest what I had just heard. Wait a minute! No one had told me we were moving. I glanced over at Linda but she seemed OK with it – smiling and hugging everybody.

I turned back to Aunt Barb and meekly said, "What do you mean we are moving - when?"

"Right now," she softly replied, "Now say your goodbyes, your dad and Margaret (our new stepmother) are waiting outside in the car." She warmly smiled and laid her hand on my shoulder, "It will be alright, go on now."

I looked over at my friends, raised my hand in a half-hearted wave and quietly said, "See ya." "See ya," they replied.

Still in a daze, I stumbled out the doors and sure enough, Dad's car was parked right out front. He was talking to Uncle Paul and Gramma. He looked over, "Get in, I will be right there."

I climbed in the back seat and just sat there staring at the floorboards. How could I have not known? Did they talk about it while I was outside or involved in other stuff? I didn't even get to say good-bye to Grampa, or Skipper, or any of my friends that were not at the church. Where was my stuff, especially my bike – they had better not give it away! No Sir, at that moment my world had just been turned upside down and I was not a happy camper. It was a pretty quiet ride to our new home.

However, Uncle Paul & Gramma showed up later with all our stuff, including my bike, and our new home was nice so I cheered up a bit.

By the time we had been in Dawson for a couple weeks, I had had a chance to check out my new home and it did have some good points going for it.

Riding a bike on pavement was way easier than riding on gravel. No longer

were our friends 2-6 km away – our new friends were across the street or just a couple of blocks away. No more riding cold school buses for two hours a day – our new school was only a five-minute walk. The cement swimming pool didn't have leaches. Hockey was played indoors – you could still play at 30 below and, of course, no shoveling snow before you played.

And let's not forget about having lights in every room, electric/gas heating – no more chopping firewood - and television. – Sure, it was still black and white but we did have three channels.

An added bonus – indoor plumbing, – no more cutting holes in the ice, no more lugging pails of water, no more washing and bathing in lukewarm water – nope, just turn the taps and lo and behold hot and cold running water. I bet you thought I forgot about the best part – no more scurrying out to the Crystal Palace outback, no more worrying about sticking to the seat in winter and no more checking for bees under the seat in the summer – now the biffy was just a few feet away, the seat was always warm and at the push of a handle everything was clean again. Yep, we were living the good life now!

I will always fondly remember those years spent with Gramma, Grampa and Uncle Paul on the farm with Aunts, Uncles, and Cousins close by. It may have been a hard life, but a simple life with family, friends and community spirit. A time spent with joy, love, and serenity – country life at its best!

But those days are now over – Linda and I were no longer country folks, no longer 'Almost Pioneers' – we were now 'City Kids' – but those are stories for another day.

"When one adventure ends another one begins"

Final Thoughts

If you are a youngster reading this I encourage you to ask your parents or aunts and uncles to tell you their stories. You might not be interested now, but sometime in the future you will be – ask your questions now – while they can still clearly recall all the things they did as a kid.

If you are a parent or grandparent – look around. You never know who might be paying attention to what you are saying and doing. Never miss the opportunity to share your experiences and pass along lessons learned. They will create new memories that will stay with them a lifetime and help guide them on their journey into adulthood.

Bailey, Brian, Dianne, Lydia

Thank you for taking the time to ride along with me as I have relived some of the most rewarding and wondrous times of my life. I hope you enjoyed reading the stories as much as I did writing them.

"Possessions come and go, but memories last a lifetime!"

One final thought – a poem. One very cold winter's eve back in the late 1990's my buddy Dave and I were enjoying a fine restaurant meal. The conversation turned to what life would have been like for the early settlers of the Peace River Region.

As I began telling Dave about my family's pioneer experiences his eyes lit up and he started to quote from Jack London's *'The Cremation of Sam Magee."* It didn't take long until we were both inspired to create our own version. I thought it might be a fitting way to end this adventure:

Songs of the Peace

Snowflakes sigh through the winter sky
Like the down of absent geese
In innocent sleep, they fall, peaceful and deep
On the breast of The Mighty Peace

The amber rays, of a low sun play
Through a grove of naked birch
The shadows of their limbs stretch thin as the hymns
That haunt an abandoned church

A hesitant doe sniffs the virgin snow
And scrapes at the frozen sod
Then she turns an ear as though she can hear
The casual humming of God

Crystal clouds lift from a silver drift
On the winter's tentative breath
They swirl and shift, in a smoky mist
As light as the Angel of Death

The cold winter night holds an opal moon's light
In the arms of a tightening vise
And with every turn sets the skies to burn
With a fire that crackles like ice

When the North wind crawls up the trembling walls
Her song is piercing and wild
Then the pioneer's hound hugs the stone cold ground
And howls like an agonized child

Beneath the painful brilliance of a clear sky's pavilion.
The Ghosts of the Peace Country sing.
In the shimmering gleam of a crystal dream
They carol the promise of spring

Though the winter cold can buffet the soul
'Till we covet a season's release
The will to survive, and the courage to strive
Accompany the Songs of the Peace

Jack Ash & David Doherty

The End'

Manufactured by Amazon.ca
Bolton, ON

33507645R00103